"What do you know about my daughter?" Tanner demanded.

Anger and desperation darkened his face. There was no doubt she'd hit a nerve.

"Your daughter?" Georgette asked.

"Don't play games with me, Georgette. You come in here in your little power suit, flash a business card that says you're from the D.A.'s office and ask me the same questions over and over." He picked up her drawings and shook them in her face. "Now you show me a sketch of my missing daughter and some muscular thug."

"I had information you were linked to the young woman in the drawing, but I never realized—"

"Is she in trouble?"

"She could be...."

His grip tightened on her arm. "Talk, Georgette!"

"If I tell you the truth, you must promise never to tell a soul."

He exhaled sharply. "I'll promise whatever you want. Just tell me how _____ Lily."

"I know because _____ ow because I have t_____

Dear Harlequin Intrigue Reader,

To chase away those end-of-summer blues, we have an explosive lineup that's guaranteed to please!

Joanna Wayne leaves goosebumps with *A Father's Duty*, the third book in NEW ORLEANS CONFIDENTIAL. In this riveting conclusion, murder, mayhem…and mystique are unleashed in the Big Easy. And that's just the beginning! *Unauthorized Passion*, which marks the beginning of Amanda Stevens's new action-packed miniseries, MATCHMAKERS UNDERGROUND, features a lethally sexy lawman who takes a beautiful imposter into his protective custody. Look for *Just Past Midnight* by Ms. Stevens from Harlequin Books next month at your favorite retail outlet.

Danger and discord sweep through Antelope Flats when B.J. Daniels launches her western series, McCALLS' MONTANA. Will the town ever be the same after a fiery showdown between a man on a mission and *The Cowgirl in Question*? Next up, the second book in ECLIPSE, our new gothic-inspired promotion. *Midnight Island Sanctuary* by Susan Peterson—a spine-tingling "gaslight" mystery set in a remote coastal town—will pull you into a chilling riptide.

To wrap up this month's thrilling lineup, Amy J. Fetzer returns to Harlequin Intrigue to unravel a sinister black-market baby ring mystery in *Undercover Marriage*. And, finally, don't miss *The Stolen Bride* by Jacqueline Diamond—an edge-of-your-seat reunion romance about an amnesiac bride-in-jeopardy who is about to get a crash course in true love.

Enjoy!

Denise O'Sullivan
Senior Editor
Harlequin Intrigue

A FATHER'S DUTY

JOANNA WAYNE

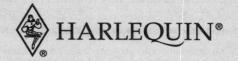

HARLEQUIN®

TORONTO • NEW YORK • LONDON
AMSTERDAM • PARIS • SYDNEY • HAMBURG
STOCKHOLM • ATHENS • TOKYO • MILAN • MADRID
PRAGUE • WARSAW • BUDAPEST • AUCKLAND

Special thanks and acknowledgment are given to Joanna Wayne for her contribution to the NEW ORLEANS CONFIDENTIAL series.

ISBN 0-373-22795-7

A FATHER'S DUTY

www.eHarlequin.com

Printed in U.S.A.

ABOUT THE AUTHOR

Joanna Wayne lives with her husband in the perfect writer's hideaway beside a lazy bayou, complete with graceful herons, colorful wood ducks and an occasional alligator. When not creating tales of spine-tingling suspense and heartwarming romance, she enjoys reading, traveling, playing golf and spending time with family and friends.

Joanna believes that one of the special joys of writing is knowing that her stories have brought enjoyment to or somehow touched the lives of her readers. You can write Joanna at P.O. Box 2851, Harvey, LA 70059-2851.

Books by Joanna Wayne

THE CONFIDENTIAL AGENT'S PLEDGE

I hereby swear to uphold the law
to the best of my ability; to maintain the level of
integrity of this agency by my compassion for victims,
loyalty to my brothers and courage under fire.

And above all, to hold all information and identities
in the strictest confidence....

CAST OF CHARACTERS

Tanner Harrison—New Orleans Confidential Agent who's obsessed with finding his missing daughter.

Georgette Delacroix—Junior prosecutor in the D.A.'s office. She's dedicated to her work and determined to deny the *gift* passed down by her mother.

Lily Harrison—Seventeen-year-old daughter of Tanner, who is running for her life.

Juliana Lodge—Lily's mother and Tanner's ex-wife.

Isabella Delacroix—Georgette's voodoo priestess mother.

Mason Bartley—Ex-con who is now a Confidential agent and Tanner's partner.

Becky Lane—Underage prostitute who supplies Tanner with information about Lily.

Sebastion Primeaux—District Attorney who is sleeping with the mob.

Jerome Senegal—Ruthless mob boss.

Tony "The Knife" Arsenault—A mob enforcer who gets out of jail on missing evidence.

Maurice Gaspard—Pimp who stays out of jail by killing anyone who'd dare testify against him.

The Scorpions—South American rebels who've infiltrated the French Quarter.

To everyone who loves New Orleans,
a sultry city with history, mystique, excitement
and a thousand faces, all uniquely its own.

Chapter One

August in New Orleans was like a nasty disease that clogged your lungs and made you sweat from every pore in your body. It was near midnight now and still there was no relief from the heat or the humidity, especially not here on the edge of the French Quarter where the stench of stale beer, fried seafood and someone's pot habit hung heavy in the air.

Tanner Harrison had loved the inner city and the French Quarter once. He'd fed on its boisterous revelry, couldn't get enough of the jazz, the food or the Big Easy attitude. That had been years ago. Now the area was like everything else in his life, a plague to be endured. But tonight desperation added a new element to his restless discontent. It rode his nerves like a hissing snake looking for somewhere to sink its fangs.

Lily. Sweet, innocent Lily. Climbing onto his lap and cuddling into his arms for a bedtime story. Skipping through Hyde Park on a summer's day, her tiny hand clutching his. Waving goodbye as he'd boarded plane after plane after plane, always turning at the last second so he didn't see the tears sliding down her cheek and she didn't see the back of his hand flick across his own wet eyes.

Only Lily was no longer living in London with her mother. And his seventeen-year-old daughter was no longer innocent.

His daughter was here in New Orleans, last seen turning tricks for Maurice Gaspard. Tanner had seen it all in a lifetime of law enforcement, but nothing had ever made him physically ill the way thinking of Lily like this did.

He jerked to attention when he spotted a young woman running toward him, her high-heeled shoes bumping and scraping along the uneven sidewalk, her long blond hair flying behind her. Her skirt barely reached her thighs and her blouse was skin-tight, a bit of gauzy material that dipped low and revealed everything short of her nipples. He braced himself and studied her face as she came closer, looking for signs of the Lily he knew beneath the layers of makeup.

It wasn't Lily, but she wasn't much older than his teenage daughter, and she was running scared. Tanner reached out and grabbed her arm as she rushed past him. She clawed at him with long, fake fingernails painted a bright red.

"Let go of me."

"Right after we have a little talk."

She twisted to see behind her, then tried again to pry his hand from her arm. "I'm not working now, so get your rocks off with someone else."

"I'm looking for Lily Harrison."

"That's your problem."

"I just made it yours, too. Lily Harrison. She's seventeen, blond and pretty, with a British accent. I know she worked for Gaspard for a while."

"Seventeen. You're sick, man. You know that? Sick. Leave the girl alone and get a life."

"She's my daughter." Tanner pulled out the picture of Lily, frayed and bent from being carried around in his sweaty pocket. He handed the photo to the woman, then tugged her under the streetlight so she could see the details. "This was taken six months ago. If you've seen her at all, I need to know where and when."

"I don't know nothin'. So let go of my arm."

But Tanner figured she did know. Like the rest of Gaspard's *women,* she was just too damned scared to talk. No one squealed on the sleazy, revengeful pimp.

"Who are you running from?" Tanner demanded.

"I'm not running. And if I was, it's none of your damn business." She threw in a few gutter words for emphasis. "Look, man. I don't know your Lily, but there's a young girl in that courtyard back there, and she's hurt bad. If you want to do something, go help her, just leave me out of it. Please, leave me out of it."

"Which courtyard?"

"Half a block down. You'll see the break between the buildings. There's an iron gate, but it's not locked."

Tanner released his hold on the young woman, then took off running. He reached the gate in seconds, pushed through it and into a courtyard illuminated only by moonlight. The victim was lying in the middle of the enclosure, sprawled across the hot concrete, one leg dangling over a fountain that was dry and green with slime.

Tanner knelt beside her and brushed the long, blood-matted hair from her face, then felt the breath explode from his lungs in relief when he realized the half-dead woman wasn't his Lily.

He checked for a pulse. It was weak, but it was there. He grabbed his cell phone and called for an ambulance. The young woman opened her eyes and stared at him.

"Don't...hit me. Please. Don't hurt..."

"I'm not the one who attacked you. Just lie still. There's an ambulance on the way."

Her face was swollen two sizes too big, her arms were scratched and bleeding and there was a long gash running across her forehead, possibly made by the cracked flower pot that lay next to her.

Tanner lifted the woman's head. "Who did this to you?"

"No one. I...fell."

"Like hell you did! Was it Gaspard?"

She shuddered and closed her eyes without answering.

"I'm looking for Lily Harrison. Do you know where I can find her?"

She didn't open her eyes or show any indication she could hear his pleas for information. Still he knelt beside her and monitored her pulse and labored breathing until the shrill cry of the sirens pierced the night.

Tanner put his mouth close to her ear one last time as he heard the footsteps of the paramedics approaching. "Do you know a girl named Lily Harrison? She's British."

The victim's eyes fluttered open as if she were trying to focus, then rolled back in her head before closing again.

"One word will do. I'm begging. Do you know where I can find Lily?"

There was no answer. Tanner moved out of the way as the paramedics loaded her onto the gurney. He had his doubts she'd live to see the hospital.

GEORGETTE DELACROIX jerked awake and sat up straight in bed, then grabbed the ringing phone. "Hello."

"Ms. Delacroix?"

"Yes?"

"This is Amos Keller."

It took her a second or two to place the name. "The ambulance driver?"

"Yes, ma'am. You asked me to call you if I picked up another beating victim who appeared to be a prostitute."

Her pulse quickened. "Yes. Did you?"

"Yes, ma'am. Picked her up in a courtyard on Chartres Street."

"How long ago was that?"

"A few minutes ago, but if you want to see her while she's still alive, you better hurry down here."

"I'll be right there. Thanks for the heads-up on this."

"Glad to help. Whoever did this deserves to be locked away."

Georgette threw on a pair of slacks and a white cotton shirt, buttoning it as she slipped her feet into white sandals. After slapping some cold water on her face, she rinsed her mouth with antiseptic mouthwash and ran a brush through her dark hair. Good enough for a predawn trip to the hospital, she decided, not bothering with lipstick.

Twenty minutes later, she was rushing through the emergency ward, looking for someone to point her to the right room. It was always faster than dealing with the admitting nurse and her legalese and protocol.

"Code blue in room twelve. Code blue in room twelve."

Georgette dodged a nurse wielding a crash cart, then followed her to room 12. A man in jeans and a blue T-shirt stepped out of the room and Georgette slipped past him only to be ushered out by a thin, middle-aged nurse with a no-nonsense expression.

"No visitors. Not now."

But the quick glimpse Georgette got of the activity in room 12 was enough to know that they were fighting desperately to save the life of a young woman who'd obviously been beaten. The clothes thrown over a hook were a good indicator that the woman had been working the streets.

Georgette had no firm evidence to back up her suspicion that the skinny, weasel-looking pimp with hair that looked like black wire dipped in axle grease was responsible for this, but odds were that he was. All she needed was one breathing, talking, witness to help her take Maurice Gaspard to trial. Judging from the sounds coming from room 12, she wasn't likely to get that witness tonight.

She studied the man slouched against the wall opposite her, the man who'd come out of the victim's room as she'd walked up. A friend? Or one of Gaspard's flunkies sent to make sure the woman didn't talk?

Georgette sized him up quickly. Early- to mid-forties. A couple of inches over the six-foot mark.

Hard-bodied. Thick, dark brown hair that could use cutting. A defiant stance.

"What happened to your friend?" she asked, nodding toward the closed door to room 12.

"She's not my friend."

"So why are you here?"

"I stumbled on her in the French Quarter after someone had beaten the hell out of her. I called the ambulance."

"And then you followed it to the hospital?"

"Are you a cop?"

"No." She put out a hand, "I'm Georgette Delacroix, a prosecutor with the District Attorney's office."

"You're working a little after office hours, aren't you?"

"I was hoping to see the patient before she…"

"Before she dies. You can say the word. It's pretty obvious she's fighting for her life in there."

"I know. I sincerely hope she makes it."

"Yeah."

The door to room 12 opened and the doctor appeared. "Is anyone here with the patient?"

Georgette stepped up.

"I'm sorry," the doctor said. "We did all we could, but we lost her. She had massive internal hemorrhaging and severe toxic shock. Basically, her body just shut down."

"Were there bullet wounds?" Georgette asked.

"No. She'd been hit over the head with a blunt object and severely beaten. I'm sure the police will do a full investigation. We'll need someone to stick around and give them and the hospital some identifying information on the expired patient."

"I'm afraid I'm as in the dark about that as you are." Georgette introduced herself and looked around for the man who'd been standing there a few seconds earlier. He was halfway down the hall, hurrying to the exit. She excused herself and chased after him.

"I'd like to ask you a couple of questions," she said, when she caught up with him.

"Ask away," he said, not slowing his pace.

"Did the victim say anything to you when you found her?"

"Yeah. She begged me not to hit her again. Evidently she was too out of it to realize I wasn't the guy who'd attacked her."

"Exactly where did you find the body?"

"In a courtyard on Chartres Street, river side, a couple of blocks off Esplanade."

"Do you live in that area?"

"No."

"Work there?"

"No. I was looking for someone. I found the victim instead."

"Did she mention her own name or anyone else's name?"

"No."

"Look, I don't know why you were down there this time of the night, and right now I don't really care. I'm not trying to prosecute you for soliciting or buying illegal drugs. I just need evidence to put the guy responsible for killing that young woman in jail."

"Isn't that the police's job?"

"Of course, but…"

"But you think you can do a better job of this than they can."

She exhaled sharply, venting her frustration. "I do

my job a little differently than some prosecutors, but I'm not trying to usurp the NOPD's authority or responsibility. I would like to have your name, just so I can contact you again if more questions come to mind.''

"It doesn't matter how many questions come to mind. I've told you everything I know." He reached in his pocket and pulled out a business card. ''But you can reach me at work if you want to waste your time. Crescent City Transports. The name and number's on the card.''

She reached out her hand to take the card. His fingers brushed hers and she was hit by a jolt that all but sucked her breath away. She dropped her hand, and the card fluttered to the floor as images played in her mind with dizzying force.

A young blond woman, face bruised, her hands and feet tied, her eyes red and swollen. And scared—very, very scared.

''Are you okay?''

The voice cut through the images, and Georgette forced herself to focus on the man standing in front of her. "What did you say?"

''You look as if you're about to pass out. Do you want me to get a doctor?''

''No, I'll be fine. I guess I've just overdone it a bit lately. Sometimes I forget to eat and my blood-sugar level dips.'' That was a lie, but she'd used it before. It was far more believable than the truth.

''Can I give you a lift home?''

''No. I'll go to the snack area and get some juice from the vending machine. I'll be fine after that.''

''If you're sure.''

''I am.''

She watched him walk away, still troubled by the force of the vision and the fact that it was somehow associated with the man who claimed to have just stumbled over a dying prostitute in a deserted courtyard.

The gift. That's what her mother called it when the psychic images took over her mind. Some gift. More like a curse from Lucifer.

She'd spent half her life trying to deny it, the other half trying to escape it. The old ways belonged to her mother and her grandmother before that. They were part of the world of chants, spells and hexes, and they had no role in the life of a junior prosecutor for the New Orleans District Attorney's office.

Still, the image preyed on her mind. She reached into the pocket of her jacket to search for the card the man had given her, then saw it on the floor by her shoe. She stooped and picked it up. The apprehension hit again, but this time without the visions or the physical impact she'd felt when their hands had touched.

Tanner Harrison. Crescent City Transports, on Tchoupitoulas Street. The guy could be as innocent as he said, but she had a very strong suspicion that he wasn't.

The gift was often confusing, but it never lied.

TANNER DIDN'T go back to the French Quarter that night. Instead he crawled behind the wheel of his sports car and drove back to his apartment, three third-floor rooms in an aging mansion on Napoleon Street. Like him, the house had seen better days.

There was no way he'd get the victim out of his mind tonight, no way he could forget the fear in her eyes when she'd begged him not to hit her again. His Lily was out there somewhere, likely facing that same kind of fear. She might have already been beaten like that, might even be...

No. He'd told Georgette Delacroix to come right out and say the word, but when it was Lily he was talking about, he couldn't even think it. He couldn't begin to understand what had possessed his daughter to fly to New Orleans and take up a life on the streets, but according to his ex, this was all Tanner's fault.

In all likelihood, it was.

The guilt settled into a gnawing pain as his thoughts shifted to Georgette Delacroix. One minute she'd been firing questions at him, the next she'd looked as if she was in some kind of trance.

She didn't look, talk or act like an attorney, at least none that he'd ever had dealings with. He'd guess her age as early thirties, and she was tall and shapely, with cold black hair that fell to her shoulders. It was her eyes that had really gotten to him, though. Dark as night, mesmerizing when she'd questioned him, haunting when she'd looked as if she might pass out on him. She was elegant, but exotic—a dangerous combination any way you cut it.

Whatever. Georgette Delacroix was not his problem and he hoped he'd never have to see her again.

GEORGETTE SAT at her desk staring at Tanner Harrison's card and wishing she'd never met the man or even touched that card. It had been three days since the night she'd encountered Tanner in the hallway at Charity Hospital. Three days since she'd first seen the images of the young woman and felt her fear and desperation.

The images had hit several times since then, appearing at the most inconvenient of times—in a meeting with the D.A., while she was taking a deposition, and in chambers with Judge Colbert this morning. Fortunately they hadn't been as intense as they'd been at the hospital, but they had been powerful enough to make her lose her train of thought and appear less than totally competent.

Tanner Harrison was somehow connected to the woman in the images. Georgette was certain of that, though she was sure of nothing else. For all she knew, the woman with her hands and feet tied and the woman who'd died in examining room 12 could be one and the same.

Or the woman in the visions could still be fighting for her life. The next victim. The possibility stewed in Georgette's mind, taking over her concentration until it was useless even to think of writing the brief she'd started a half dozen times over the last few days.

Tanner Harrison, innocent employee of Crescent City Transports? Or, Tanner Harrison, lynch man for the mob? Murderer of young women who crossed the lines Gaspard drew in invisible ink?

She picked up the card and felt a cold, frightening shudder slither along her spine. To play this safe and according to protocol, she should take her fears to the police.

But what would she tell them? That she saw visions? That some unnamed woman was calling to her for help? Let that get back to her boss and District Attorney Sebastion Primeaux would fire her before she could open her mouth to deny it.

But neither could Georgette go on like this. So, it

was field-trip time. She'd pay a surprise call on Tanner Harrison, but this time she'd stay in full control while she questioned him. A junior prosecutor on her way up should never have her equilibrium shaken in public.

Georgette planned to make it to the very top of the heap.

Chapter Two

Tanner hung up the phone; he'd been talking to the New Orleans Chief of Police as his newly assigned partner stopped at the door to his office.

"Guess you heard—another tourist died last night from a drug overdose," Mason Bartley said, leaning his long, lanky body against the door frame.

"Yeah, I just got off the phone with Henri Courville."

"What did the police chief have to say?"

"That the victim was a sixty-five-year-old retired guy from Champagne, Illinois, in town for a model railroaders convention."

"Evidently got off on the wrong side of the tracks," Mason said, "and ended up facedown in a back alley in the Quarter."

Tanner nodded. "Which is exactly how I'd like to leave Maurice Gaspard some night."

"Watch it, Harrison. You're starting to sound like me."

He sure as hell hoped he wasn't. Mason had been a two-bit crook up until a few months ago, when he was recruited to join the top secret New Orleans Confidential agency. And while the boss might think he was rehabilitated, Tanner had serious doubts. He'd griped for two days when Conrad Burke had made them partners in this high-stakes case. A lot of good it had done. Burke hadn't budged an inch.

"We've closed the coffeehouses the mob's used as distribution points, shut down the refining operations for their illegal sex drug, and locked the doors to the plush gentleman's club where they were drugging the johns and robbing them blind through theft or blackmail. And still we have guys ending up in the hospitals and the morgue from heart attacks brought on by an overdose of Category Five."

"Ain't no stopping them," Mason said.

"We'll stop them—one way or another." And that's what he liked about being an agent for New Orleans Confidential. They played by different rules than agencies like the FBI or CIA. The Confidential agents answered only to Conrad Burke and to their own conscience.

"We've slowed them down," Mason admitted, "which means their supply of Category Five has to be running low. But the head pimp Maurice Gaspard is out on bail and still running his underage girlie show with the help of his heavies." Mason walked over and dropped the file he was holding on top of Tanner's desk. "Burke said to give this to you. It's the autopsy report on that prostitute you found the other night with her skull crushed."

"Courville said they got a positive ID on her last night," Tanner said. "Samantha Lincoln, runaway from some town in Iowa. Age sixteen."

"Sixteen. Those slimeballs. Got no conscience at all." Mason turned and stared at the framed picture of Lily sitting on the top of Tanner's file cabinet.

"Don't guess you've got any leads on the whereabouts of your daughter yet?"

"No. Hard to get anyone to talk when the price of squealing is death."

"If she's out there, you'll find her."

The empty consolation did nothing to dissolve the acid pooling in the pit of Tanner's stomach. It had been two months since Lily had disappeared, and he'd gotten nowhere in his search. He couldn't go on like this, trying to do his job for New Orleans Confidential when all he could think about was the fact that Lily was out there somewhere, maybe hiding out in some stinking crack house, just trying to stay alive.

He'd thought when they got Tony Arsenault off the street that the mob would loosen its hold. But Jerome Senegal apparently had no shortage of thugs to do his bidding. Tony the Knife and his infamous machete were in custody, but whether a person was sliced by Tony or beaten by another mob enforcer didn't matter a whole lot. Dead was still dead.

Tanner let the report slip from his fingers, walked over to the file cabinet and picked up the photograph of Lily. It had been taken last Christmas—yet another holiday he'd missed sharing with her....

The intercom on his phone buzzed. He replaced the picture and lifted the receiver. "What's up?"

"You have a visitor in the main building."

"Who?"

"Georgette Delacroix."

Not the best of news. "Did you tell her I was in?"

"No. Thought I'd check with you first, but if it sways your decision, Susie said she's a knockout."

Yeah, and an attorney. If that wasn't bad enough, she'd gone freaky on him the other night, practically passed out in the hospital. Avoiding her was tempting, but on the other hand, if he played this just right, he might pick up some info from her.

It was always advantageous to get a little inside scoop on happenings in the D.A.'s office, especially now that they suspected the corrupt prosecutor was in Senegal's back pocket. They'd get Sebastion Primeaux when the time came. It wasn't here yet.

"I'll walk over," Tanner said. "Is there an office available?"

"The usual. I'll tell them you're on your way."

Crescent City Transports was a legitimate trucking business that served as a front for the Confidential operation. Confidential's offices were in the back and security-controlled, supposedly because they handled some hazardous materials as well as a few routine transports.

As far as any of the regular employees knew, the Confidential agents were garden-variety employees like themselves, and while they were aware they drove specially outfitted vehicles, they had no idea that the equipment consisted of the best surveillance technology money could buy. The back building was strictly off limits to regular personnel or visitors.

Tanner grabbed his blue one-piece driver's uniform from the hook on the back of the door and slipped it on over his jeans and shirt. As far as Georgette Delacroix was concerned, he was just a truck driver.

GEORGETTE FOLLOWED Tanner Harrison down the hall, already feeling an unexplained shudder of apprehension, though so far the images of the blond woman hadn't returned. He opened an office door about midway down the hall.

"We can talk in here."

She stepped past him and into a room that, unlike Tanner, was warm and welcoming. There was a highly polished conference table in the middle of the room, surrounded by large wooden chairs with padded leather seats. Framed black-and-white prints of New Orleans landmarks hung on three walls, and a table beneath a row of windows held a coffeepot and white mugs.

"Would you like some coffee?" Tanner asked. "Or I can get you a soda if you'd rather have that."

"No thanks." She set her handbag on the table and slid onto one of the chairs. "Crescent City Transports must be a new company. I haven't heard of them before."

"We're new and successful, but I'm assuming you're not here because you want something transported."

"No. I have a few questions about the woman you found beaten in the French Quarter."

"I told you all I know."

"Could you tell me again how you found her?"

"I stumbled over her like I said. She needed help. I called for an ambulance."

"I visited the crime scene. It was through a narrow, gated passage between two brick buildings. Seems as if it would be difficult to stumble that far off the street."

"I heard moaning and checked it out."

"Most people wouldn't have in that section of town. They might have called and reported it to the cops, but they wouldn't have gone down a dark passageway on their own."

"Guess I'm not like most people then."

"You said you were looking for someone. Who?"

"I'd hoped to hook up with some friends in the Quarter that night. I didn't, so I was walking back to my car. End of story."

"The problem, Tanner, is that this isn't the beginning or the end of the story. May I call you Tanner?"

"Sure, *Georgette*. Call me whatever you like. It won't alter the fact that I've told you all I know. Now why isn't that the end of the story?"

"The woman you found isn't the first prostitute to die this way."

"Newspaper this morning said she was number five."

"At least. Five young women who should still be alive. We have to stop this needless killing, so if you know anything at all, please share it with me."

"I wouldn't have any reason not to tell you."

Unless he was involved in this. She looked into his eyes. They were gray, cold and daunting. Tanner slid into the chair next to hers and her throat constricted, making it difficult to swallow. Even without the images, the man had a disturbing effect on her.

"You want to tell me why you're really here?" he asked.

"I just did."

"You're not a cop. You're a lawyer, and I'm not involved in one of your cases."

"Then why do you think I'm here, Tanner?"

"You think I had something to do with the beating, and that if you keep harassing me I'll blurt out the truth. But since you're not a cop, I guess you're just looking to pick up a big case and acquire some clout. Best of luck with that, but you're still wasting your time with me."

"This isn't about clout. It's about underage girls being sucked into a life of prostitution and being killed if they try to leave."

"If you know that much," he said, "why don't you and the NOPD go in and shut down the operation? You surely know that mob boss Jerome Senegal and his second-in-command Maurice Gaspard are behind all of this."

"Whatever information we have is privileged at this point."

"Sure and you'd tell me, but then you'd have to kill me." He leaned closer and something inside her head clicked on, releasing a rush of adrenaline and an out-of-breath feeling, as if she'd been running.

"If you attorneys with the D.A.'s office are so gung ho on getting the bad guys off the streets, quit throwing out the cases and take more of them to trial."

"Everyone is innocent until proven guilty. We can't take people to court without sufficient evidence to warrant it."

"Well, you're not going to find any evidence here, and I've got to get back to work."

Just as well. Although she felt strong, disturbing vibes around Tanner, the images she'd expected hadn't returned and she was getting nowhere with her questions. She opened her leather briefcase, took out her business card and laid it on the table between them. "If you think of anything else, please call me."

"Nothing else to think of."

Only he didn't get up to leave. Instead, he picked up her card and studied it as if it were a puzzle he was trying to solve. "I guess you've questioned a lot of prostitutes," he said.

"A few."

"They must be running scared these days what with the attacks."

"Some are."

"What do they do when they get scared? Do they band together? Leave town? Have someone who helps hide them?"

"It varies."

His questions suggested more than casual interest and reinforced Georgette's original fears about Tanner. His gaze bored into hers, and the intense scrutiny stirred confusing emotions.

"I appreciate you taking time to talk with me," she said, standing and extending her hand.

He took it, and she felt a rush of warmth, followed by needling prickles along her fingertips. The images of the young blond woman returned, full force, pushing reality aside.

Perspiration rolled down Georgette's forehead and mud squished between her toes. There was nothing but endless swamp in front of her and the air was so fetid, it made her nauseous.

She reached out for something to hold on to as her knees buckled and she started to slide into the murky water, but all she caught hold of was the open briefcase which crashed to the floor at her feet.

"Hey, don't faint on me."

The voice sounded as if it were coming from a long way off. Finally, the images began to evaporate, leaving Georgette shaken, but aware that Tanner had an arm around her shoulder and was holding her steady.

She jerked away. "I'm sorry."

"No need to be sorry, but you need to see a doctor."

"I'll be fine."

"You damn sure don't look it, and you totally blacked out for a few seconds there."

She raked her hair back from her face and took a couple of deep breaths. The images had faded, but the fear hadn't let go of her. Fear so intense it was palpable, but it didn't belong to Georgette. It belonged to a young woman. The same woman as she'd seen in the psychic visions the other night, but her hands and feet were no longer tied, and this time she was running through a swamp.

"Let me get you a soda," Tanner said, already stooping to gather the papers that had apparently slipped from her briefcase.

"Thanks." That would buy her some time. Besides, her throat was so dry she could barely swallow. Tanner was definitely involved with the woman in some way. So now what? She couldn't question Tanner about the images, and she certainly couldn't take this to Sebastion. One hint of the gift, and she'd lose all credibility, if not her job.

But when Tanner returned and she took the cold soda from his hands, she felt the strange connection take hold again. Someone was trying to reach Georgette through Tanner.

Or else the evil emanated from him.

"I WANT HIM out of jail—now."

Sebastion Primeaux stared past Jerome Senegal and kept his gaze on the barge floating down the Mississippi River. It was late afternoon, but the sun was still relentless, and the humidity felt as if they were breathing through wet wool.

"I can't let Tony walk, Senegal. The media will be all over me."

"You're breaking my heart here, Sebastion. I thought we were friends. Friends don't let friends down."

"I've done everything you asked up until now, but this is over the line. It'll cost me my job and then it won't matter if you blackmail me with those damn pictures or not."

The mob kingpin stepped into Sebastion's space, his breath reeking of garlic. "Does it matter if one of my guys pays a visit to that pretty little wife of yours? Does it matter if he slices up that face right in front of your kids?"

Sebastion felt the pressure pushing against his brain.

"So what is it, Sebastion? Tony or your wife?"

"Leave my family out of this, you—"

"What? You giving the orders now?" Senegal smirked, and his leathery face screwed into a thousand rutted wrinkles. "'Cause I don't think you got the balls to go against me, Sebastion."

And if he did, Jerome Senegal would cut them off or have one of his hit men do it for him. Meet Senegal on the street, and he was just another guy in his late fifties who'd eaten too much jambalaya and crawfish and spent too much time baking in Louisiana sunshine, but Sebastion knew him for what he was.

He'd earned his right to run the mob by killing anyone who got in his way, had beat their brains out with a baseball bat and had their bloody bodies delivered to their front door like some deranged Christmas package.

Sebastion turned around, half expecting to see someone climbing up the levee swinging a baseball bat, but there was no one there but them. Just two guys standing on the levee out near Bridge City, watching the Mississippi River roll by.

"Give me a day or two," Sebastion said. "I'll see that Tony's released."

"I knew you'd see things my way, but we don't have a day or two. He's got to walk today."

Although Senegal didn't spell it out, Sebastion knew the mob boss needed Tony to set up a new drug refining operation since the last lab had been shut down by the cops.

"There's no way I can do what you ask."

"Sure there is. It's all taken care of. You just play your little part when Judge Boutte calls and asks to see the evidence."

"I don't have the evidence. It's at the courthouse in the evidence room."

"I've got that under control. Can you handle your part of the deal?"

"You don't leave me a lot of choice."

"Glad you see it my way. Now I've got to run. Tell your wife and kids hello for me."

Sebastion watched him walk away, hating him, hating himself, too, for being stuck in a situation that could only get worse. Most of all, he hated that there was no way out.

IT WAS one of the rare times when all the New Orleans Confidential agents were gathered in one room, and, as usual when that happened, Conrad Burke was not smiling.

He shuffled some papers while the group poured themselves cups of the dark chicory coffee from the pot on the back counter and found chairs around the round table. Just like the knights of old, only they were out to slay scorpions instead of dragons. And there wasn't a white horse in sight.

Alexander McMullin was second in command to Burke. Young, cocky, a risk taker who'd grown tired of the rules that went along with being a cop. He was perfect for the Confidential team. Seth Lewis was even younger, only twenty-nine. He was a homeboy who had joined the army to see what the world looked like outside the ghetto. Now he was fighting a different kind of war.

Tanner was the old man of the group. Forty-three. He'd seen enough to know that he liked his cars fast, his jazz cool, and his women hot—and temporary.

He also knew this was the first job he'd had in a long time that he could sink his teeth into, the kind of no-rules operation he'd been looking for all his life.

"It's been a long, hot summer."

Tanner refocused on the meeting as Burke got down to business.

"I've got a feeling it's about to get even hotter, but before I hit you with that, I have some good news. Wiley Longbottom is making great progress. He's being released from the hospital but is staying in town a couple of weeks longer so that his cardiologist can keep a check on him."

They broke into applause. Everybody loved the retired director of the Colorado Department of Public Safety, and had been worried sick about him.

"Wiley got us off to a great start in New Orleans," Burke continued. "He became one of the drug overdose victims of Category Five and launched us into war against the mafia drug trade and ring of underage prostitutes. We've had some successes there, though not enough, but we haven't made any headway with the original assignment. We still don't know why the Nilia rebels who support the overthrow of their democratic government are in New Orleans.''

''Are we sure Scorpion Poison hasn't left the area?'' one of the agents asked. ''We haven't spotted any of the members in almost a week.''

''Not only are they still here,'' Burke answered, ''but the Coast Guard and CIA think illegal substances were smuggled into New Orleans yesterday on a cargo ship that was docked in Miami at the same time a ship from Nilia was in that port. Something big is up. We need to find out what that something is.''

''Any ideas what we should try next?'' Mason asked.

''I'm standing in front of the best idea and action bunch I know. Now it's up to you guys. Do what you have to do, but get this job done. I expect a hundred percent of your efforts, and unless you're eating or sleeping I expect a hundred percent of your time. Just remember, if the game goes sour, there's no such agency as the Confidential. You are on your own.''

The room grew quiet, not because that bit of news came as any surprise. They'd all been made aware of the rules of engagement up-front. The silence was more a reflection of their moods. So far they'd found out nothing about the rebel presence in the city, and failure in any form was not acceptable to the men in this room. Everyone except Tanner would give the assignment a hundred and ten percent.

Their daughters weren't missing.

''I'll be meeting with each of you one-on-one over the next few days,'' Burke said. ''In the meantime,

I'd like you to give serious thought to your next plan of action.''

There were a few more questions, but the meeting was basically over. Burke was a family man. He and his wife had twins only eight months old, but he never asked his agents to do anything he wouldn't tackle himself. He'd be out there in the fray with them, putting his life on the line in the same way he expected them to be.

There wasn't a man in the room Tanner wouldn't trust with his life—except one—and he was walking toward Tanner right now.

"Party time," Mason said, smiling broadly. "I say we go out and kick some Nilia rebel ass, partner."

"First we have to find them."

Tanner's cell phone vibrated. He took it from the clip at his waist and stepped out of the room to take the call.

"Hello."

"Hello, Tanner."

He recognized the strident voice with the heavy British accent immediately. His ex. Talk about making his day.

"Hello, Juliana. I was going to call you later."

"Don't lie to me, Tanner. You weren't going to call. And I just want one thing from you. Have you found my daughter?"

"*Our* daughter. I haven't found her."

"You thought you were such a bloody good CIA agent, so why can't you find your own flesh and blood?"

"I'm trying."

"You better be. This is all your fault. If you'd been

a halfway decent father, you'd know where your daughter is.''

All his fault, but then what hadn't been? ''I'm doing everything I can to find her, Juliana. It's just a matter of time.'' He doubted she believed him, wasn't sure he believed it himself any longer.

She spouted more accusations, and his grip tightened around the phone. There was no reasoning with Juliana when she was like this. There would be less reasoning if she knew that their daughter had been working as a prostitute.

She started a new round of accusations, and he held the phone away from his ear. It had been ten years since he'd lived with her, yet that screeching voice could still set every nerve in his body on edge.

''I'll call you later. And I won't rest until I find Lily. I promise you that.''

Juliana broke into tears, then hung up the phone without saying goodbye. He probably hadn't said the right things today any more than he'd ever managed to say the right things two times in a row when they were married.

A rotten husband. A lousy father. Par for the course.

The door to the conference room opened and the guys started filing out, all fired up and ready to go out on the streets and do their job. He could see it in their eyes and the way they walked, shoulders back oozing confidence. Only one thing on their minds, the way it had to be if you were a Confidential agent. It was the promise they'd given, the one he'd given, too. But that was before his world had been turned upside down.

He waited until Burke walked out, then joined him. ''I'd like to talk to you if you've got a minute.''

"Sure thing, Harrison. Let's go to my office."

Tanner nodded, and kept walking, feeling sick inside, as if he were about to walk off the edge of a cliff with nothing to break his fall but jagged rock.

There was no cliff, but he was about to do the second hardest thing he'd ever done in all his life. And once again, there would be no going back.

Chapter Three

"Is this about Lily?" Burke asked as he closed the door.

"Am I that transparent?"

"You are now that I know what it's like to be a father. Hope this doesn't mean you got bad news."

"No news. I comb the Quarter every night, ask questions, search the crack houses and dark alleyways. There's no sign of her, and if anyone knows where she is, they're not talking."

"I won't even claim to know how hard this must be on you, Tanner. If there's anything I can do…"

"I don't know what it would be. I'm not even certain she's in the area anymore."

"You want to sit down?" Burke asked.

Tanner shook his head. "I'd rather just say what I have to say and go."

"Why do I have the feeling this isn't something I'm going to like hearing?"

Tanner exhaled slowly, tempted to walk away and let things ride, but it wasn't fair to anyone, most of all Conrad Burke. "You said you expect a hundred percent from all of us. I've got no quarrel with that. It's the pledge I made when I signed on with you.

But I can't give it. I spend at least half my time searching for Lily. That's just the way it is right now. I don't think I can change that."

"You wouldn't be the kind of guy I'd choose for my team if you could."

Tanner stuffed his hands in his pockets. This was tough, but putting it off wouldn't make it any easier. "You need every man pulling his weight. I'm not pulling mine. I don't know what else to do but resign from New Orleans Confidential."

"Is this what you want to do?"

"No. Hell, no! I want to be out there. I want to be in the thick of the action. I want to get Senegal and Gaspard so bad I can taste it. And I want to be on the front line when we take down those scorpion-tattooed gorillas."

Burke drew his lips into a straight, taut line and nodded slowly. Tanner felt the finality of his association with Burke and the Confidential team burn in his gut.

"It's my loss," Tanner admitted, "but finding my daughter has to come first."

"We need you on the team, Tanner. I specifically picked you for what you have to offer. You're tough and tenacious and loyal to the core."

"I could come back when this is over, when I know Lily is safe."

Conrad shook his head. "No. This isn't the kind of situation a man can drop in and out of. You're one of us or you're not."

"I understand."

"I don't think you do, Tanner. I'll lose a good man if I have to, but not like this, especially when I don't see your searching for Lily as a problem. While you're out in the streets and crack houses and dark alleys looking for a lead on Lily, just keep your eyes and ears open for information on the Nilia rebels. I know you're already doing that.''

"You're sure?'' Tanner asked, not wanting a reprieve now only to have to deal with this later.

"I'm sure.''

"The other guys may have a problem with it.''

"I doubt it, but if they do, they can take it up with me.''

"What about Bartley?'' Tanner asked.

"What about him?''

"I'm not going to be able to keep an eye on him all the time if I'm out searching for Lily.''

"I didn't pair Mason Bartley with you for you to keep an eye on him.''

"Didn't you?''

"No. I hired him because I believe he's the man for the job.''

"A leopard doesn't change his spots.''

"That's true of leopards, but men can and do change.''

Burke threw his arm around Tanner's shoulder. "Do what you have to. In the end, that's the measure of a man.''

"Thanks.'' Tanner's fears for Lily were just as strong as he walked over and opened the door, but the clenching in his stomach had eased. He was still a Confidential agent. He was still a member of the team.

LILY HARRISON leaned against the trunk of a cypress tree, so weak she could barely stand. She was hot and tired and so very hungry. She'd kill right now for fish and chips the way Bertoli's on Edgeware Road made them. All crispy and golden. And water, clean, cold water that was fit to drink and not this murky mess she was standing in.

She closed her eyes and pretended she was back home in her own bed where the sheets always smelled of lemon and the down duvet was soft as a cloud.

Something swished in the ankle-deep water and she forgot the dream and took off running again. It was more difficult now. Her legs ached and her lungs burned as if someone were holding them to a torch, but she couldn't stop, couldn't let the two monsters catch her. Dying in the swamp, even being eaten by alligators, would be far better than the way they'd kill her.

She'd give anything to have never hopped on that bloody plane to New Orleans. To have never gotten caught up in the underage prostitution ring that had led to her witnessing that grisly double murder in the back alley of the bordello. Now Lily was fleeing for her life from two mob hit men, and she feared it was only a matter of time before they caught up with her again.

Something sharp dug into the heel of her right foot. The pain went all through like some kind of electrical charge. Tears burned and slid down her cheeks, but she managed to hold in the scream that tore at her throat.

All she'd wanted to do was come to the States and get to know her father. But Mum had been right. America was a frightening place. And her father didn't want her in his life. That hurt a hundred times more than the pain and fear that was driving her over the edge.

And still she ran, fighting to stay a step ahead of death at the hands of madmen.

GEORGETTE SAT UP in bed and clutched her chest. She couldn't see anything in the blackness of the room, but she could hear sucking noises behind her, footsteps in the swamp, coming closer and closer.

She kicked at the sheets, and all but fell out of bed before reality checked in enough that she could regain her equilibrium. She reached for the lamp and flicked it on, knocking over a glass of water she'd left on the bedside table.

She grabbed a handful of tissues and soaked up the water, though her mind was drifting back to the nightmare she'd been caught in minutes ago.

The same young woman who'd been haunting her while she was awake had now taken over her mind while she slept. Georgette had dealt with these crazy psychic experiences all her life, but never had they come at her with this frequency or intensity.

She wondered if this was what it was like for her mother and grandmother. Had they once fought it the way she did, only to finally give up and accept this as part of their lives?

No. Her grandmother maybe, but not her mother. Isabella Delacroix embraced the gift like a lover. It was Isabella's life. It would never be Georgette's. Yet Georgette couldn't shake the fear as she walked to the kitchen and poured herself a glass of milk. She'd walked away from the gift every time before, but something was different this time.

Her mother would probably know why. But asking her mother would mean going back to the house she hated and admitting that the curse was claiming control over at least part of her life.

She took her milk to the balcony. Her condominium was on the top floor of a converted warehouse just a few blocks off the Mississippi River. The view from the balcony was magnificent, but all Georgette could see tonight was a swamp and a young blond woman running for her life.

Damn the gift and damn Tanner Harrison for forcing this on her. If he was involved with this young woman in any way, she'd find out and she'd make him pay. She'd find out at any cost.

Which meant that, as much as she dreaded it, she'd have to make a visit to Isabella Delacroix.

"YOU GOT A DOLLAR, mister? I haven't had anything to eat since breakfast, and I'm real hungry."

"Hungry, are you?" The guy took the dirty hand Becky held out to him and pulled her beneath the streetlight. He shoved her mass of thick, black curls away from her face. "What's your name?"

"Are you a cop?"

"A cop? Whatever gave you that idea? I'm a businessman, and I may be able to help you."

"Hmmp. Not a lot of people looking to help me, but my name's Becky Lane."

"Are you from around here?"

"What's that got to do with anything. I stay here now."

"I see. Do you have any family here?"

"You sure ask questions like a cop."

"I can assure you that I'm not in law enforcement." He looked her over, from top to bottom and up again. "You may be exactly the kind of girl who can do well in my business."

Becky studied the man, afraid of what he might really want from her. He was a honky, tall and skinny, with slicked-back black hair that looked as if he'd soaked it in motor oil. The man gave her the creeps, but he was dressed nice, and she was hungry.

"I just need a few dollars or whatever you can spare," she said.

"What you need is a job, so you can buy your own food and some nice clothes. A young lady has needs."

"What kind of job are you talking about? I'm not a hooker, you know."

"A hooker? Such a disgusting term. I don't deal in disgusting. I deal in class."

"How old would I have to be to get this job?"

"Eighteen would be old enough. You look eighteen to me."

She was barely sixteen, though she did look eighteen when she wore lipstick and had her hair fixed. She didn't mind lying about her age, as long as he didn't want some kind of proof. "I'm eighteen, but I don't have a driver's license or anything like that."

"You won't need to drive in this job." He led her to the circle of illumination beneath a streetlight, then tugged on her blouse, pulling it to the back so that the fabric fit tight around her breasts. "You have a nice shape and nice skin," he said, stroking her cheek with the back of his hand. "Men like light-brown skin when it's as soft as yours. We'd have to do something with that hair, of course, and you'll need decent clothes, something expensive. Have you ever worn silk?''

She didn't answer, just stared down at her worn, dirty jeans and stained sneakers.

''I'm talking high-class, Becky. Very high-class. No gutter talk. No gutter clothes. No gutter ways. Just high-class dancing, and being friendly. You're a friendly girl. I can tell. This will come naturally to you.''

''When would I start?''

''We'll talk about that later. In the meantime, let me take you to see a friend of mine. She'll see that you get a good meal and have a nice bed to sleep in tonight. The rest of this can wait until tomorrow.''

Food and a bed. She wasn't about to turn that down. As for the job, she'd make up her mind about that later. ''What's your name?'' she asked.

''Mr. Gaspard.''

''That's a nice name.'' And so far he seemed like a really nice man. She hadn't met too many of those. Maybe New Orleans would be the place where her life got turned around for good.

GEORGETTE PARKED her beige sedan in front of the shotgun house in old Algiers. Some guys next door were working on their car in the street, their jeans hanging so low on their hips, she could see the band of yellowed underwear at their waist. They were shirtless and shoeless, and one was gulping down a can of beer.

He finished it, crushed the can in his hands and tossed it to the curb as she got out of the car and started up the front walk to her mother's house. Some parts of old Algiers had experienced a rebirth over the last few years. The historic old houses had been restored and the yards and streets cleaned up. They'd started neighborhood watches and gotten rid of the run-down vacant houses frequented by addicts looking for a place to flop.

A neighborhood like that would have tossed Isabella Delacroix out.

The old feelings were potent as Georgette climbed the front steps and knocked on the door. It had been over a year since she'd seen her mother and then it had been at a café in the Quarter at Isabella's request. It had been five years since Georgette had been in this house. That had been the night her grandmother had died.

Georgette lifted her hand to knock again, then dropped it to her side. She couldn't do this. She absolutely couldn't be drawn back into curses and *gris gris* and mysterious spells. She turned and had reached the steps when she heard the door open behind her.

"Georgette."

Her mother's voice crawled under her skin the way it always did. It was lyrical and haunting, as much a part of who and what Isabella was as the bright colors she wore and the bracelets and earrings that jingled when she walked.

Georgette took a deep breath, then turned to face her mother. "Hello, Momma."

"Come in, Georgette. Please. It's been so long since I've seen you."

Georgette looked for words but didn't find them, so she just walked to the open door and stepped inside. Isabella hugged her then stepped away and started straightening some magazines on a small table.

The house hadn't changed. The front room was where her mother did business. Telling fortunes, reading tarot cards, giving psychic advice. As always, it smelled of incense and spices, and was dimly lit by lamps whose shades were draped with red silk cloths. Music played in the background, an aria from an unfamiliar opera.

"Come with me," Isabella said. "Let me look at you under the bright light."

Georgette followed her into the small kitchen at the back of the house. It was exactly the same as it had been five years ago. The appliances were old but clean, and the small wooden table and chairs were the ones Isabella had bought in a second-hand furniture store on Magazine Street when they'd first moved here from down the bayou.

Charcoal drawings Georgette had done in high school were thumbtacked to the wall next to the refrigerator, and an eight-by-ten framed picture of Georgette in her cap and gown hung on the wall behind the table. It had been taken the day she'd graduated from Tulane Law School.

Isabella ran her fingers through Georgette's shoulder-length hair, then cradled her cheeks in her hands as if she were a small child. "You are so beautiful. You look like your grandmother did in her old pictures. You have the same hair. Silky and black as pure onyx."

"You have the same hair, Momma."

"Maybe once. I don't remember. Are you hungry? I could fix us some lunch. I have an appointment at two, but nothing before then. That gives us a whole hour and a half to visit."

Far more time than Georgette planned to be here.

"I'm not hungry," she said, "but fix something for yourself if you like. We can talk while you eat."

"I'll eat a bite later, but I'll make us some herbal tea. It's good for the tempers."

They didn't talk as Isabella filled the kettle and adjusted the flame on the front burner of the gas range. When she finished with that, she dropped two tea bags into a teapot and took two delicate china cups from the cabinet.

"I wish you'd come to see me just because you wanted to," she said, taking the chair closer to Georgette, "but I think it's something much darker that brings you here."

"It is." Georgette spread her hands on the table. "I've been seeing images of a young woman who appears to be in danger."

"Is it someone you know?"

She shook her head. "I've never seen her before."

"What do you see in the revelations?"

"The first time she had her hands and feet tied, but last night she was in a swamp. She's running. I think someone must be chasing her but I only see the young woman."

"She's calling out to you."

"Then why aren't things clearer?"

"It's the way of the gift. It only shows what it wants to show. When did the visions start to appear?"

"A few nights ago. I'd gone to the hospital to see a prostitute who'd been assaulted. She died while I was there."

"So you think the images are tied to the victim?"

"I'm not sure. The first time they appeared was when I talked to the man who claimed he had found her and called an ambulance."

"You sound as if you don't believe him."

"I don't know what to believe. I saw him again a few days later and the images returned."

"Do the images only materialize when you're with this man?"

"No. Last night…" Her voice trailed off as the images shadowed her mind.

"What happened last night?"

"I had a nightmare. I was running through a swamp and when I woke my heart was pounding so I was afraid I might have a stroke or a heart attack."

"You are experiencing her fear."

"So what do I do to make the images stop?"

"Find a way to help the woman."

"How can I? I don't know who she is or where she is."

"Go back to the man and tell him what you see. Demand that he tell you the truth."

"I can't do that, Momma. I'm a junior prosecutor. I can't go around telling people about visions. They'll think I'm …"

"Crazy as me?" Isabella reached over and put her hands on top of Georgette's. "If I could have, I would have spared you this anguish, Georgette, but withholding the gift isn't within my power. You have it. You must learn to live with it."

The teakettle started to whistle. Isabella went to the range and poured the water over the two tea bags. Her long skirt swayed with her hips and the charms dangling from at least a dozen bracelets jingled with every movement of her arms.

Isabella was fifty-one, eighteen years older than Georgette, but she could have passed for mid-forties. She was striking, with dark eyes and thick black lashes that set off her soft brown eyes. She possessed all the beauty traits Creole women were famous for, and yet Georgette knew her mother never saw herself as pretty.

Not that she saw herself as ugly. It was just that Isabella lived on a different plane. She saw things no one else saw, but she never saw herself. She just took her looks the way she took life, as if it were in control and she was there to do its bidding.

Isabella set the teapot on the table and settled back in her chair. "Maybe you're not giving the visions a chance, Georgette. You can't fight them or try to push them away. That only thwarts the power that lies inside you and keeps you from seeing things clearly."

"I don't want to see any more, Momma. I want you to tell me how to make them stop."

"And what about the young woman?"

"She's not my responsibility. I didn't ask for any of this. I refuse to let it claim my life."

"It's not so simple, my sweet one. You can't choose when the gift shows itself or when it goes, but you must listen to it."

"Why? Why do I have to pay attention to something that has no place in my life?"

Isabella took her hands in hers. "Look at me, Georgette. Look into my eyes and listen carefully to what I say. If you deny the gift and ignore the images you may be sentencing this woman to death. And if you do that, her blood will be on your hands and it will never go away. Never."

Isabella put her hands in front of her, staring at them as if she could actually see blood running between her fingers and dripping onto the floor.

The room grew icy cold and Georgette longed to

bolt and run away, but something held her. "Did you ignore the gift and let someone die, Momma?"

"It doesn't matter. The past can never be undone. Tell me about this man who first caused the images to appear."

"His name is Tanner Harrison. He's a truck driver, I think. He doesn't have a criminal record. I checked. But I have this feeling that he's not leveling with me."

"You must be careful, Georgette. Be very, very careful."

"Then you think he's dangerous."

"All I know is that sometimes when the images are so strong that they won't let you go, the danger can reach out for you, too."

"What should I do, Momma? Please. You must tell me."

"Talk to this man. Spend time with him, and go where the images lead you."

"Are you saying I should go into a swamp and look for her?"

"It might help. All I know for certain is that you must let the visions guide you. Follow them, but don't let your guard down. Not for a second."

The tiny kitchen seemed to be closing in on Georgette, and she hated that she was here, that she was talking of spells and curses and psychic visions. Hated that her insides were tumbling around and making her nauseated. Hated that she'd been sucked back into a life she'd tried so desperately to escape. "I don't want to talk about it anymore."

"You're right. I've probably said enough for now."

Even Isabella seemed relieved to let the subject

drop. Georgette drank her tea, then said a hurried goodbye. If she were half-smart, she'd go back to her office, bury herself in her work and not give any more thought to the blond woman in the swamp. She'd pretty much convinced herself to do just that when she turned on the radio and heard the latest news.

A young woman's body had been pulled from the Mississippi River in Plaquemine Parish. She'd been identified as Simone Billings, a prostitute who'd been listed by her friends as missing a month ago.

...her blood will be on your hands.

Isabella's warning echoed in Georgette's mind as a new plan formed in her mind. Swerving into a U-turn, she headed toward Tchoupitoulas Street and another visit with Tanner Harrison.

Chapter Four

Tanner had spent half the night searching for leads, and he was bone-tired when he got the message that Georgette Delacroix was in the front office of Crescent City Transports and asking to see him—again. For some reason the news didn't surprise him, maybe because the exotic beauty with the strange habit of blacking out on him had been on his mind far too often since she'd swayed against him in the conference room.

One of the weird things about being a man. No matter what was on your mind, your libido could come into play at the first touch of a seductive woman's body. But Georgette had concerned him more than she'd aroused him. Something was going on with her, though she obviously wasn't going to explain it to him.

Whatever her reasons, she was zeroing in on him, so once again Tanner grabbed his uniform from the hook on the back of the door and went off to meet the intriguing and very inquisitive attorney.

GEORGETTE LOOKED UP when Tanner walked into the conference room.

"We've got to stop meeting like this," he said, offering a half smile that didn't reach his eyes.

"I won't keep you but a minute."

He looked at his watch as if he were going to time her. "How can I help you?"

"I seem to have lost a notebook, and I thought perhaps it fell out of my briefcase when I was here the other day."

"If it did, I didn't see it. I can check in the office to see if anyone's turned it in."

"Thanks," she said. "I'd appreciate that."

"So what are we looking for? Small? Large? Some kind of binder?"

"Letter-size with a black leather cover," she lied.

"Make yourself at home. I'll be right back."

She slid onto one of the chairs and opened her briefcase. She'd scribbled some notes after driving over, mostly impressions from the nightmare. She couldn't tell Tanner about her visions, but her operational plan involved more than a fictitious notebook.

If Sebastion found out about this, he'd raise all kinds of hell, scream that she was overstepping her bounds and that she should be spending her time concentrating on the cases she had going to trial. But then Sebastion was frequently in a foul mood these days even if she didn't give him reason to complain.

Georgette pulled out the pencil sketch she'd done in the parking lot before coming inside to see Tanner. It was a recognizably close match to the young woman from the visions. Long straight hair, petite, probably no more than a size four. Big eyes. Full lips. Light brows, not too thick. A classic nose. Face slightly oblong, almost regal. And very young. Now all she had to do was study Tanner's reaction when he saw the drawing.

But while she was sitting there, a new image flew into her mind. This time it was a dark-haired, Hispanic man with slicked-back hair and tattoos all over his biceps.

She started to draw, filling in the features, her fingers flying as she transferred his likeness to the page, so lost in what she was doing that she didn't hear Tanner when he walked up behind her.

"What do you know about Lily?"

The pencil dropped from Georgette's hand and rolled to the middle of the table. She turned and stared at Tanner. Anger darkened his face and clamped his jaw tight. There was no doubt she'd hit a nerve.

"Lily?"

"You know damn well who I'm talking about." He reached behind him, hooked the door and slammed it shut. "The girl in the picture. Where is she?"

"You're asking me?"

He grabbed her arm and tugged her to her feet. "Don't play games with me, Georgette."

"I'm not playing."

"So what do you call it? You come in here in your little power suit, flash a business card that says you're from the D.A.'s office and ask me the same questions over and over." He picked up her drawings and shook them in her face. "Now you show me a sketch of my daughter and some muscular thug."

His daughter. Surely not, but when she met his gaze and saw the distress in his eyes, she was almost sure he was telling the truth.

"I didn't know she was your daughter."

"Why else would you be here with this picture?"

"I thought…" She caught herself before she blurted out too much. "I had information you were linked to the young woman in the drawing, but I never realized…"

"I don't give a damn what you've heard about me. I'm only interested in one thing. Do you know where Lily is?"

She shook her head. "Not exactly."

He tapped his finger on the burly ruffian she'd drawn. "Is she with this guy?"

"She could be."

His grip tightened on her arm. "Tell me what you know about Lily, straight, none of your attorney double-talk."

He was angry, demanding. She didn't blame him, yet even now she wasn't certain he was totally innocent in any of this. "How long has it been since you've seen your daughter?"

"Three years."

Her suspicions swelled again.

Tanner dropped to a chair. "It's not the way it sounds. Her mother and I are divorced, and Lily lived in London with her until a little over two months ago. She left there without telling me or her mother her plans. By the time I found out she was in New Orleans, she'd disappeared."

"Your daughter flew all the way from London to New Orleans but didn't contact you, not even after she'd arrived?"

"I was out of town and no one knew how to reach me. I've been searching for her since the day I got back. The only information I've been able to uncover is that she worked for Maurice Gaspard for a while."

"As a prostitute?"

"So it seems."

The pain pulled at his voice, and in spite of her doubts her heart went out to him. "I'm sorry, Tanner."

"I don't need your sympathy. Just give me answers."

He was desperate for the truth, but there was no way to tell him what little she knew without explaining how she knew it. Georgette Delacroix, junior prosecutor with the D.A.'s office. Georgette Delacroix, psychic, with the ability to see things and feel things when there was no logical explanation for her powers.

...her blood will be on your hands.

"I need to get some air."

"You're not going to run out on me, Georgette, not until you level with me."

She held on to the back of the chair with one hand and struggled for a deep settling breath. "I don't know exactly where your daughter is, but she's either in a swamp or has been in one recently. I think she's running from someone."

"Where did you get this information?"

"A source."

"Who?"

"I can't say."

He put a hand under her chin and forced her to meet his gaze. She trembled at the intensity of his anguish, but if she told him the truth, everything she'd worked for could be lost. Her career. Her chance to lead a normal life.

But if she kept her own dark secret safe, Tanner's daughter might lose her life.

The curse of the Delacroix women.

"Talk, Georgette. South Louisiana is covered in swamps. I have to know more."

Her insides quaked. "If I tell you the truth, you must promise never to tell a soul."

He exhaled sharply and for a second she thought he'd say no. Finally, he released his hold on her and let his arms fall to his side. "I'll promise whatever you want. Just tell me how you know about Lily."

She looked away from him and stared out the window, unwilling to let him see how this was tearing her apart.

"I know because…" Her voice faltered. "I know because I have the gift."

TANNER STOOD THERE, staring, while Georgette spun a tale that rivaled something from a late-night horror flick. "You actually expect me to believe that you fall into trances and see visions of Lily?"

"I'm not asking you to believe anything. I'm telling you the truth."

He started to tell her he didn't believe a word of it, but talking of this had transformed her from confident, intimidating attorney to someone who looked as if she might shatter and break at any moment. She picked up her briefcase as if she were ready to leave.

Tanner planted himself in front of the door. "You can't tell me something like this and then walk out."

"I have to go."

Dammit. Her soft brown eyes were moist and she was shaking. The last thing he needed was to let her get to him. "Stay and talk to me," he said, this time keeping his voice calm.

"Why stay if you don't believe me?"

"I'm trying, so work with me. You say you have visions, but they only go so far. What do you have to do to nudge them up a notch?"

"It doesn't work that way."

"Explain how it works."

":The trances come at will."

"There must be more to it than that."

"No. I have no control over them. If I did, I'd never experience them at all. It's not as if I enjoy being a freak."

"When did you first have visions about Lily?"

"The night I ran into you in the hospital. You seem to be the link that joins me with Lily," she admitted.

"We're together now. Are you feeling anything— or seeing anything?"

"No."

"Then we'll stay together until you fall into another trance, or get the gift, or whatever you want to call it."

"I can't do that. I have to go back to the office."

"I'll go with you."

"No."

He was losing patience fast. "It's not like we have all the time in the world, Georgette. Hours count. Hell—minutes count."

"Even if we're together, the visions may not return."

"But there's a better chance that they will. You said it yourself. I'm the link." He took her hands in his. "I'll beg if that's what you want. Just help me find Lily."

She shuffled her feet, moved her gaze from him to her briefcase and back again. "Tomorrow's Saturday. We can spend some time together then."

"That won't cut it. I don't see a ring on your finger so I'm guessing you're not married."

"That has nothing to do with this."

"It makes it easier for us to spend the weekend together."

"I can't spend the weekend with you."

"You can't spare one weekend to save a young woman's life?"

She sighed, and he knew he was getting through to her. Great. He'd have hated to have to kidnap her.

"What is it you want from me, Tanner?"

"The same thing you wanted from me. Information. Is there anything we can do other than spend time together to improve the likelihood you'll have another vision?"

"Location might help."

"You mean, if we were in a swamp."

"Perhaps. I don't really know, Tanner. I've always tried to avoid the visions before."

"We can start out tonight," he said. "Drive south and find some swampy area and see what happens."

She looked as if she were about to protest again. He didn't give her a chance. "You need me to keep your psychic powers a secret, Georgette. Well, I need something from you, too. So, give me your address. I'll pick you up at seven."

"There are no guarantees this will work, Tanner."

"But it could, and I've tried everything else."

"Okay. At seven." She scribbled her home address and phone number on the back of one of her cards and handed it to him. "It's a condominium complex in the Arts District. I'll meet you out front."

He opened the door for her. She hurried past him, as if she couldn't get away from him fast enough. He watched as she headed down the hall and to the elevator—her lustrous black hair caressing her slender shoulders, that gray suit skirt ultra conservative but still short enough to show off her shapely calves.

Not the kind of woman you'd expect to utter talk of visions and psychic powers. Whether she was on the up-and-up or this was some kind of dirty scheme, he had no choice but to go along. They were linked together by a daughter he barely knew but would do anything in his power to keep safe.

His thoughts stayed with Lily as he ducked out of the main building and walked back to his own office. He'd find her. And then he'd tear out Maurice Gaspard's heart with his bare hands and feed it to the rats in the streets.

SEBASTION'S OFFICE DOOR was open a crack. Georgette knocked lightly. "Do you have a minute?" she asked, when he looked up from the manila file folder he had open in front of him.

"Sure, come on in. Actually, I was about to see if you were back. I wanted to talk to you before you left for the weekend."

"What about?"

"A problem, but let's hear yours first." He closed the file and pushed it to the front edge of his desk.

"It's the disposition from Sara McManus."

"Is that the Griffith murder trial?"

She nodded. "Sara changes the details every time she tells her story. The defense is going to rip her to shreds if I put her on the stand."

"Isn't she your only witness?"

"Yes, but the evidence stands by itself. We don't have to have a witness."

"Do you think she actually witnessed the murder?"

"Absolutely."

"Why?"

"She gets so upset when she describes the actual stabbing that it's impossible not to believe her."

"That's your answer, Georgette."

"Then you think I should put her on the stand."

"It's your call. It's a matter of whether or not you trust this particular jury."

"Thanks for the input." Sebastion was an excellent prosecutor, and she was constantly learning from him. "One other question."

"Shoot."

"Have you ever heard of a man named Tanner Harrison?"

"Why?"

"He's the man who called the ambulance for the prostitute who was beaten to death a few nights ago."

"Never heard of him, but I never trust the innocence of a dog who's hovering around a fresh kill and chewing on a bone."

"Kind of what I've been thinking, but...never mind. What was it you wanted to talk to me about?"

"We have a problem."

Dread hit like a fist to the abdomen. Tanner had promised he wouldn't say anything to anyone about her secret, but suppose he had? She swallowed hard, but stood her ground. "What's the problem?"

"It's with a case you're working on, the one against Tony Arsenault."

Relief flooded her senses, but it was short-lived. Sebastion had that drawn look he got when things weren't going to suit him. That happened a lot these days.

"The case is going well," she said. "The evidence from the drug lab raid is so convincing we're sure to get a conviction."

"Tony's been released from jail."

"What?"

"Judge Boutte released him without bail. He says we have insufficient evidence to hold him. I have his order right here." He rummaged through some papers on his desk. His elbow brushed the folder he'd been looking at when she'd come in, knocking it to the floor. She stooped to pick up one of the sheets of paper that had sailed out of his reach.

"A science project I'm helping my son with," Sebastion said, taking the paper from her and quickly stuffing it back into the folder.

"Looks like the work of a professional."

"School requirements are tough these days." He handed her the order from the judge.

She read it carefully, growing more aggravated by the second. "It says here the evidence is missing."

"The woman in charge of the evidence room at the court house couldn't produce it."

"That sucks, and I don't buy for a second that it's lost. Intentionally thrown out, but not lost. The report in our files says that Tony's handprints and DNA were all over the drug lab—not to mention he was at the scene of the crime."

Sebastion tugged on the collar of his white dress shirt as if it were choking him. "We *had* the report."

"What does that mean?"

"I couldn't produce the file today when Judge Boutte demanded to see it."

"Are you saying that our file is missing?"

"I searched for two hours. I couldn't find it."

Everyone knew Judge Billy Ray Boutte was in Jerome Senegal's back pocket. His part in this didn't surprise her, but the missing paperwork from their office did.

"How could the evidence be missing from Tony's file? It was in a locked file cabinet in a locked room. No one removes material from the evidence files without checking them out. Whose name is last on the list?"

Sebastion nailed her with a penetrating stare. "Yours, Georgette. The entry was dated five days ago."

"I checked it out, but I put it back, Sebastion. I'm sure of it."

"I believe you," he said, propping his elbows on the desk and tenting his fingers.

"Someone else must have looked at it after that," she said. "Perhaps they're misfiled."

"They're not misfiled. I had Shirley and Jackie go through all the file drawers." Sebastion tilted his head as if he needed to study Georgette or the situation from a different angle. "The media's going to be all over this. We're going to look incompetent at best, in Senegal's camp at worst."

Of course, the media would howl. Tony Arsenault, known killer, mob executioner and drug peddler on the streets again when there had been practically an airtight case against him. But she was certain she'd returned the evidence to its proper place, and inanimate objects didn't get up and walk out on their own.

"Is it possible that we could have one of Senegal's

plants in this office?'' she asked, knowing Sebastion would balk at that suggestion.

"It's very unlikely, but I plan to look into this further."

"And in the meantime, Tony Arsenault is back on the streets." She didn't try to hide her exasperation.

"It's not as if he's the only criminal walking around free in this town, Georgette. There are any number of unsolved crimes."

Which was nowhere near a justification for letting Arsenault walk. She glanced at her watch. It was three hours until Tanner Harrison would show up at her door.

"I'm not blaming you, Georgette, but I can't promise the media won't. You'll have to hang tough."

"Sure. I'll do that." She turned and walked away, heading down the hall to the room where evidence files were kept.

Apprehension consumed her as she skimmed the files, looking for something that Shirley and Jackie might have overlooked. She rifled through each drawer, letting her finger slide across every tab.

By the time she reached the last of the Zs, she was more frustrated than ever. One step forward. Two steps back. She went back to Tony's file. It was all there except the evidence needed to implicate him in the big drug lab raid a few weeks ago.

Now he was on the street again. Free to peddle more drugs and brutally kill more teenage prostitutes who didn't do his bidding.

A shiver climbed Georgette's spine, and she trembled at the urgency that seemed to push from somewhere inside her. But the urgency didn't seem connected to Arsenault. It was all about Lily Harrison. Time was running out for her.

"WHERE'S LILY?" Tony asked.

"Lily's of no consequence. I didn't get you out of jail to deal with an English brat who doesn't know enough to keep out of business she doesn't belong in."

"I don't like the idea that a girl who can finger me is still breathing."

"She's not going to be fingering anyone, but I don't want her killed yet."

"Why wait?"

"Her father is Tanner Harrison. He's ex-CIA. I don't know what he's up to now, but I don't trust him for a minute, and I may need his daughter as a bargaining chip."

"So where is she?"

"At the duck-hunting camp."

In the swamp, where Jerome liked to have his most secret powwows. "Who's with her?"

"Butcher and one of Gonzalez's men."

"Butcher's a has-been. He doesn't have the stomach to be a hit man these days."

"That's for me to decide," Jerome said. "Lily's in good hands."

"You keep those foreigners hanging around and the feds are going to move in on you."

"That's why I need you back at work. No drugs— no money. No money—no deal."

"You got me a place to set up operations?"

"An old warehouse on the river. It's been empty for a couple of years. The raw product's already there. I just need you to make it street-ready."

"When do I start?"

"Yesterday would have been late."

"No problem. I'll have you cookin' by day after tomorrow."

"Good."

Jerome left a minute later. Tony was glad to see him go. It was his first night out of the slammer. He needed some action. One phone call to Gaspard and he'd send over some nice little number to take care of Tony's immediate need. Then he'd be on his way to the duck camp hidden away in the Atchafalaya Swamp.

Jerome might want Lily alive, but Tony wanted her dead. Cut up into little bitty pieces and dropped into the river.

He'd have to get by Butcher and the scorpion-tattooed rebel who was with him first, but they were expendable. Tony didn't have his weapon of choice— the machete had been confiscated during the drug raid—but a nice hunting knife would do. Or maybe he'd use his pistol, the way he had the night Lily had spotted him taking out that smart-mouthed bartender and Madam Dupree.

Lily had to die. Butcher and the rebel would be lagniappe.

TANNER HAD JUST HEARD the news of Tony the Knife's release when he drove up in front of Georgette's building. It pissed him off big time that the D.A.'s office had let another criminal back on the street. He wasn't surprised at the action. They'd found out a month ago that Sebastion Primeaux was being blackmailed by Senegal.

He'd like to hear Georgette's take on the latest development, but he'd have to play this carefully. He needed her help in finding Lily, but he didn't want her finding out he was a Confidential agent. The New Orleans Chief of Police knew the agents were operating in his area, and there was speculation among the local mafia that there was an outlaw band of law-enforcement personnel on the scene.

But if anyone in Senegal's organization, especially Gaspard, found out that Tanner was part of that group, it would make Lily even more of a target than she already was.

Georgette walked out the front door at three minutes before seven, looking only a little less formidable and no less attractive in a pair of jeans and a white shirt than she had in her stark gray suit.

So this was it. Tanner was off for a weekend with a sexy psychic with an attitude. It was the last thing he'd ever have expected to be doing with his time. And once again it hit him how desperate he'd become.

Chapter Five

They crossed the Crescent Connection and took Highway 90 west out of New Orleans, driving almost to Morgan City before turning off on a narrow road bordered on both sides by swampland. It wasn't quite dark yet, but the shadows had deepened quickly once they'd left the highway.

They'd talked little and the silence had been awkward between two people who barely knew each other and had no real basis for a relationship. The odd thing was that though Georgette didn't fully trust Tanner, she wasn't afraid of him.

If she'd had to explain it, she'd have said it was the pain in his eyes when he talked of Lily. No matter what else he might be, he was worried sick about the daughter he admittedly barely knew, and that touched her in a way few other things could have.

Tanner turned onto a deeply rutted dirt road and stopped in front of a cypress-shingled cabin that was little more than a silhouette in the deep purple of twilight. The cabin stood on piers and there was a shell walkway from the road to the front steps.

"Where are we?" Georgette asked.

"The cabin belongs to one of the foremen at work,

a Cajun guy named Walter who'd rather hunt and fish than eat.''

"That's good, since I don't know what else you'd do out here. As for me, I'm partial to eating and I haven't since breakfast.''

"I stopped at a deli before I picked you up. There's food in a cooler in the trunk.''

"You think of everything.''

"I try. We can spend the night here if we want. Walter said there are clean sheets for the beds and most of the essentials are on hand.''

"Essentials? Would that include running water and indoor plumbing?''

"Yeah, but he said the water tastes like iron. I brought some bottled water.''

The thought of spending the night in the isolated cabin made her uneasy. "I agreed to visit a swamp, but I wasn't planning on sleeping in one. I was thinking more like a motel—separate rooms.''

"I didn't bring you out here to jump your bones, Georgette. I just thought this might be conducive for…for whatever it is you do.''

"They're called psychic visions, Tanner. I don't *do* them. I *have* them, and you don't have to talk about them as if they're some disease that you're going to catch if you acknowledge it.''

"I didn't mean it that way.''

"Forget it. We're here, so we may as well go inside and take a look around.''

"You better spray some of this on you first.'' He reached to the seat behind them and pulled a can of insect repellent from a small zippered case. He handed it to her, then reached back and retrieved a large flashlight. "Watch your step when you get out,'' he warned. "Walker says he sees a lot of water moccasins out here this time of the year."

"What fun." She opened the car door and searched the road for anything that might be slithering around the car before stepping out. No snakes in sight, but a hungry mosquito started to feast on the back of her neck. She swatted at it, then yanked the top off the can of repellent. The lid slipped from her hands and bounced and rolled its way into a water-filled ditch along the side of the road.

"Don't worry," Tanner said, already rounding the car and catching the escaping plastic in the beam of his flashlight. "Better to lose the lid than the repellent."

Much better, she decided as another mosquito targeted a spot on her right cheek. She coated every inch of exposed flesh, then passed the repellent to Tanner. An owl hooted overhead, joining the chorus of what must have been thousands of tree frogs.

She was surrounded by mosquitoes, snakes, frogs...probably alligators as well. And somewhere in a swamp much like this one, Lily Harrison, fresh from London, was likely lost, all alone and running for her life—or maybe not. Georgette shuddered and prayed for a sign that Lily was still alive as she followed Tanner up the narrow walkway.

The fickle, despicable gift was silent.

TANNER STOOD on the back porch of the cabin and looked out at the still bayou, his muscles flexed, aching to do anything except stand here and stare into a fetid swamp.

He leaned against the post that supported the overhang, lost in his thoughts, but still aware of Georgette's soft footfalls on the creaking wooden floor. She pushed through the back screen door and joined him on the porch.

"The cabin's not as bad as it looked from the outside," she said. "Rustic, but clean."

"Only one bedroom."

"But there's a couch."

"Does that mean you want to stay here?"

"Not particularly, but the atmosphere seems right. The smells, the sounds, even the dratted mosquitoes."

"But no visions?"

"Not yet." She sat down on the top step and stretched her legs in front of her. "Tell me about Lily."

"Like what?"

"Whatever pops into your mind."

"She's seventeen. Pretty. Smart. A good kid but always had a mind of her own."

"And obviously extremely spunky if she took off and traveled to America without you or her mother knowing about it."

"Spunkier than I would have guessed. According to her mother, Lily took the money she'd gotten for her seventeenth birthday, bought a plane ticket and made the trip without telling anyone except her best friend where she was going. It was a week before Juliana found out that Lily had flown to New Orleans."

"Is that when she called you?"

"She tried. I was away on business."

"Don't you have a cell phone?"

"It was out of commission," he said bluntly. "Besides, I definitely didn't expect any news like that."

Not to mention that at the time he'd been struggling

with the fact that his plans to fly to London had been abruptly cancelled. Juliana had told him Lily no longer wanted him at her party or in her life.

"How did Lily get mixed up with Gaspard?"

"Probably the same way the other underage girls got sucked into his prostitution ring. She was in a strange city. She didn't know anyone and her money must have been running out."

"And you have no idea why she's on the run?"

"No one who works for Gaspard is going to talk, but I'm sure she crossed him—or wanted out."

"How old was Lily when she went to live in London?"

"Seven."

"You must have missed her very much."

Missed her. The words seemed so trite considering the hell he'd gone through. No morning kisses from his angel. No squealing when she'd jumped from the diving board into the neighborhood pool. No more stories at bedtime and good-night hugs.

Tanner dropped to the steps beside Georgette. "I'd have missed my right arm less."

Georgette scooted closer. "And now it must be like that for you all over again."

Crazy, but he felt as if she might really understand what this was like for him. "Have you ever had a child?"

"No. I'd never chance passing the gift down to a child."

"You'll miss out on a lot."

"I thought so before now. After seeing how upset you are, I'm sure it's not worth it."

"Oh, it's worth it, all right. I just should have been a better father."

"I don't know what happened between you and your daughter, but Lily's trying to reach you, Tanner. She's speaking through me to connect with you."

"So where are the damn visions now, Georgette?" he asked, feeling as if he were being eaten alive with frustration. "We're together and in the swamp, so where are they now?"

The minutes ticked by, long pregnant minutes with nothing but the sounds of the bayou to break the silence. Something splashed in the water behind the house, likely a fish or perhaps an alligator crawling from the bank into the slow-moving water.

Georgette stared straight ahead, but her body grew taut, and the muscles in her face and neck were strained. Tanner felt a surge of adrenaline push through his veins. He didn't understand this psychic bit and still only half believed it, but he'd seen Georgette fall into the trance-like state before. He knew she was on the verge of doing so again.

She winced as if she were in pain, and her breathing became shallow and quick.

"I can't keep running. I can't. It hurts so bad. *Daddy!*" Georgette's scream echoed through the night.

Tanner slipped an arm around her shoulder and pulled her close. Minutes later, Georgette went limp, but it was several minutes before she spoke. "I saw her again, Tanner. I saw Lily."

"Is she still in the swamp?"

"Yes, I don't think we're in the right area. She seemed far away. She wasn't running this time. I think she was lying down."

Panic shot through him. "But she was breathing?"

"Yes. And calling for you, but there's no way to

tell about the timing. Sometimes visions hit in real time, but not always.''

''What does that mean?''

''They could be from the past—or the future.''

''Then just tell me what you saw.''

''Lily was lying on wet, muddy ground, only this time...'' Georgette held tight to his hands. ''This time she wasn't alone.''

''ARE YOU hurt?''

Lily stared at the man standing over her. He was so old his face seemed to have fallen into his chin. His clothes were dirty, and he smelled of cigarettes and sweat. But he wasn't wielding a knife or a gun, and, whoever he was, he had to be better than Butcher or Raoul.

''I'm lost,'' she said, afraid to tell the truth until she knew if this man could be trusted. ''I guess I must have fallen asleep.''

''You lucky to be alive, you.'' His accent was heavy Cajun, like some of the people she'd met in the Quarter.

''How did you find me?'' she asked, scanning the area, still having difficulty believing that her kidnappers were not nearby.

''I was fishing the bayou and I heard someone screaming 'Daddy'.''

The scream that she'd never meant to escape. ''Thanks for stopping to help.''

''Your Daddy the one what lost you, huh?''

He was staring at her, his eyebrows arched, waiting for an answer. If she told him the truth he'd probably leave her there. She wasn't his problem, and there was no reason for him to risk facing two killers for someone he didn't know.

"My daddy was fishing. I wandered off. When I tried to go back to him, I must have gone the wrong way. Do you have a mobile that I can use?"

"A mobile?"

"A cellular phone."

"Ain't got no phone. No use for one."

"Then maybe you could take me to a petrol station so that I could call for help."

"You talk funny. Where you from?"

"London, England."

"You a long way from home, you."

"I'm living in the States now. In New Orleans. I just need to get back to town."

"I don' go to the city, me. I drop you off at the highway. You hitch a ride, huh?"

"Yes. That would be great."

"You hungry?"

"Very hungry and thirsty."

"I got some water in the pirogue. And some crawfish stew back at the house. You eat, then you go to town."

She nodded thankfully. She'd tried not to think about how hungry she was, or how thirsty, but now that he'd mentioned it, the need for food and water consumed her.

He reached out a hand.

She took it and let him help her up, but when she put weight on her right foot, she yelped and fell back to a sitting position.

He stooped and lifted her foot. It was coated in mud and dried blood. The man took a knife from his pocket and scraped the flesh. Pain shot through her body as if he'd jabbed her with the point of the blade.

"Didn't mean to hurt you, but you got the infection. Nasty, it is, eh?"

She bent over to get a closer look, then shuddered. The whole foot was red and swollen and she could see pockets of pus beneath the filthy skin.

"What you think you walk on that?"

"I hoped I could."

He picked her up and heaved her across his bent shoulders like a sack of potatoes. He was stronger than he looked, and he carried her across the boggy earth and deposited her in his narrow wooden boat.

He stood instead of sitting, and pushed them away from the bank with a long pole. "What's your name?"

"Lily."

"Like the flower."

"Yes, like the flower. What's yours?"

"Folks call me Crazy Eugene."

"Why do they call you crazy?"

"Cuz I am. Not all the time. Just some a d'time. Folks know to stay away from me then. You don' need be scared, you. I don' never hurt no women."

Maybe he didn't, but Butcher and Raoul had no qualms about it, and she was certain they were somewhere nearby, searching for her. They wouldn't give up until they'd found her—or until she was dead.

She'd have to take her chances with Crazy Eugene and a foot that needed medical attention. Take her chances and hope she hadn't just fallen into another form of hell.

Her mother would be frantic with worry and angry with Lily for leaving home. But her mother didn't understand how much it had hurt when her father hadn't come for her birthday.

All I wanted was for you to love me, Daddy. Because I never stopped loving you.

"YOU ROTTEN piece of..." Tony let the curses fly. Whatever he called Butcher, it wouldn't be bad enough. "How could two grown men let one unarmed teenage girl escape?"

"Don't get your bowels in an uproar. It's not like we planned it. She broke out a bathroom window and ran. Not that she'll get far in the swamp. She's a city girl. Got no swamp sense a'tal."

"How long has she been gone?"

"I dunno. Couple of hours. You think I just sit around here and stare at the clock?"

"I hope not. Be a shame for a man to have nothing better to do on the last day of his life."

Butcher pulled a switchblade from his pocket and flashed the blade. "Don't mess with me, Tony. This ain't your show."

"It is now that I'm here to run it."

Sweat beaded on Butcher's forehead, and his Adam's apple jumped around as if he had some kind of tic. Senegal kept him around cause he was a distant cousin, but Tony had never had any respect for the guy.

"You hit the whiskey, didn't you, Butcher? You and that Scorpion rebel probably passed out like some frat boys on a binge and let Lily Harrison get away from you."

"You don't know nothin'. Raoul's out there tracking her down. He'll be back here with her any second."

Butcher had likely lied about how she got away. Probably lied about how long she'd been gone, too, but instead of trekking through the swamp looking for her, he was sitting high and dry in the cabin as if he didn't have a care in the world. At least he had been until Tony showed up. Now he was sweating bullets.

"You ever smell fear on yourself, Butcher? If not, take a big whiff. 'Cause I smell you from clear over here."

"I ain't scared of you. You kill me and Jerome will take you down."

"I don't see Jerome around nowhere right now. Don't see Lily, either, and that's the problem. No British bitch is going to finger me on a murder rap. And no fat slob like you is going to get by with letting her escape."

Butcher backed away. "I'll go help Raoul look for the girl. Senegal wants her alive, but you're the one she saw do the hit, so I figure it's up to you to do what you want."

"Nice of you to see it that way." Tony reached for the scabbard strapped across his thigh and pulled out the jagged-edged hunting knife.

Blood rushed to his brain, the thrill of the kill surging through his veins. One quick slice of the jugular. Or a surgical removal of the heart. That's why he liked a knife—or a machete. So much more personal and satisfying than a bullet.

But Butcher was lagniappe. It was Lily he needed. And killing Butcher now would only give him one less man for the search.

"Get out of here, Butcher. And don't come back without Lily."

Butcher took off running.

Tony dropped to the worn couch that smelled of cigarettes, booze and sweat. He could really use a joint, but he had to stay focused. He'd give them a couple of hours on their own to search for Lily, but if they hadn't found her by then, he'd go out there and find her himself.

There were a million places to hide, but Tony knew this swamp better even than Crazy Eugene. After all, Eugene had raised him.

GEORGETTE SAT across the small wooden table from Tanner, picking at the chicken salad he'd brought for their dinner. There were buttery croissants as well and fresh kiwi and summer peaches. All they needed were candles and soft music, and this would have had all the trappings of a romantic evening in the bayou country.

But they were not lovers, not even close. Still she was linked with him as intricately as if they had been. They were joined by their need to save his daughter, but there was a heady sensual awareness hovering between them as well. He was far too virile for her to be alone with him in such an intimate setting and not be cognizant of him sexually.

In another situation, he would have likely been far more daunting, but now all she could feel was his desperation. He'd do anything to find his daughter. All men weren't like that. Some could walk away from their own flesh and blood and never look back. Some fathers just didn't care at all.

"Hope it's not the chicken salad that's causing that look of distress on your face," Tanner said.

"No. I was just thinking."

"About Lily?"

"Indirectly."

"What we need is a landmark," Tanner said, "a road sign or a person's name, or even the name printed on a boat. Anything that would give us some clue to go on."

"I have no control over what appears in the images."

"Yeah. I know. So we just sit around and make small talk." He pushed back from the table. "I'm sorry, but this isn't cutting it. I'm better off on the streets asking questions than I am waiting for some psychic revelation that leads nowhere."

"I'm ready to go back to the city when you are."

He crossed the room and stared out into the black depths of a moonless night. "Maybe we should try taking the boat down the bayou first."

"It's pitch-dark."

"I've got a flashlight."

She'd never been in a swamp at night before and the thought of venturing out in this one gave her the creeps. She imagined water moccasins slithering through the water. And alligators that were probably longer than the boat they'd be in.

"We won't go far from the cabin," Tanner said. "But if you're on the water, out there with the sounds and the smells, maybe the visions will intensify and give us something solid that we can sink our teeth into."

She shuddered, suddenly hit with a terrifying premonition that if she said no, the images would desert her. She swallowed hard, felt a throbbing in her fingertips, then looked down and realized she was clutching the edge of the table.

"Okay, Tanner. But after that, I want to go back to town to my own apartment. We can try this again tomorrow, but I need to be in my own bed tonight." The tough prosecuting attorney tone she'd strived for didn't come through, but Tanner didn't object.

He merely grabbed his baseball cap, plopped it on his head and strode out the back door. Apprehension swelled to something almost palpable as she followed him into the blackness.

"Boy, did you tag it right. He's got her wrapped around his little finger. Make you sick to see them. They're at some old bayou cabin in the swamp a few miles south of Morgan City."

"Just the two of them?"

"Yeah."

"Sonofabitch."

"Want me to take care of the situation?"

"Only if you can pull it off exactly as we talked about. I don't want any mess-ups."

"You think I can't handle Tanner Harrison?"

"He's not a pushover."

"Trust me. He'll be alligator bait by midnight."

Chapter Six

Becky twirled in front of an antique mirror, admiring her body beneath the folds of red silk. Only problem was the skirt was too short and the top was too low. She tugged at the bodice, trying to get it to cover more of her breasts.

"What are you doing?" Mary Ellen asked, laughing at Becky's attempts. "You'd better show as much as you can."

"And have guys pawing at me all night? No, thanks."

"There won't be any pawing tonight, at least not out in the open. This is a high-class affair."

Becky dropped to the couch and slipped her freshly pedicured toes into the new red stiletto-heeled sandals. "Where is this affair?"

"In an elegant French Quarter pied-à-terre."

"Who'll be there?"

"Some of Mr. Gaspard's clients and the other ladies who work for Mr. Gaspard," Mary Ellen replied.

"Me? A lady?"

"You look like one now. And you better act like

one. If you don't, you'll be back on the streets and jobs like this don't show up every day."

"I still don't know exactly what kind of business Mr. Gaspard's in," Becky said.

"It's associated with the tourist industry."

Becky was still skeptical. "So what do we do? Show groups around the French Quarter."

"Not exactly. It's more personal than that. You make rich visitors feel welcome."

Becky tried to stand in the shoes, then fell back to the couch. Her skirt inched up to her you-know-what and she was getting more suspicious by the minute about this job. "Are all these rich visitors men?"

"Yes, but don't worry about it. They're very nice. Besides, you don't have to do anything tonight but stick close to me and mimic what I do." Mary Ellen lifted her long, shiny blond hair and let it fall back onto her shoulders. "You'll be learning the ropes from a pro."

"Are you sure this isn't just about having sex with dirty old men?"

"Nothing dirty about it."

"Then what's it like? What is it you really do?"

"I entertain very nice men in an intimate way. Last week I had strawberries and champagne with a guy in his hotel room and all he wanted to do was watch me undress. He never even touched me."

"A pervert. But some guys must want you to do all kinds of nasty stuff."

"You have a trashy mouth on you. You probably should go back and live on the streets in those filthy clothes you had on when you came here. Eat leftovers from the garbage."

"Better than being a hooker." But she did desperately need a job. Maybe one of Mr. Gaspard's clients would hire her to work for them in an office.

Becky tried walking in the shoes again. "I'll probably get nosebleed from the altitude," she said, "and bleed all over those rich tourists."

Mary Ellen laughed. "You are so funny, girlfriend. Haven't you ever worn heels before?"

"Not this high. I don't have a pilot's license."

"You better practice. You don't want to fall on your face tonight. You know, you've got great legs."

Becky staggered back to the mirror. The shoes did make her calves look sexy, kind of like one of those models in the magazines at Walgreen's. "I could probably get used to this life if it weren't for the men."

"Gotta take the good with the bad."

"If I'd been willing to do that, I wouldn't have had to run away from home."

GLIDING DOWN the bayou in the dark was every bit as scary as Georgette had imagined it would be. The temperature had dropped a few degrees since sundown, but the humidity was still oppressive. "What's that?" she asked, shuddering at what sounded like a baby's shrieking.

"A screech owl."

Tanner kept rowing, and the small boat moved almost soundlessly through the still water. The boat was the only thing that was silent. "I never imagined the wetlands would be so noisy," she said, as a bullfrog croaked and was answered by a chorus of his fellow frogs.

"Swamps teem with life."

"I'd feel better if it were light enough to see what's

in the water with us. Is that an alligator swimming just in front of the boat?''

"It's a nutria. There are about a half dozen of them.'' He shone the light on one of the rat-like creatures. "But there's an alligator a few feet to our left.'' He swept the beam of the flashlight across the surface of the water, outlining the bony head and the tail, all that was visible above the murky water. The animal was at least nine feet long and seemingly impervious to their company.

"Thanks for sharing that with me.''

"You've surely seen alligators before. You were raised in Louisiana, weren't you?''

"How did you know that?''

"You look Cajun, or Creole, and you have a slight accent.''

Tanner was very observant. Few people took her for Creole, though she was half Creole. "I grew up in the country south of Lafayette, but we never fished or hunted or went out in the swampy area. It was just my mother and I, and we stayed close to home. What about you?''

"I'm originally from Chicago, but I've lived in New Orleans off and on for the last twenty-five years. I've spent a lot more time on the streets than in the swamps, though.''

"Yet being out here in the dark doesn't seem to get to you the way it does to me.''

"I'm not worried about nutria or 'gators. It's rats, maggots and scorpions that get to me, the human kind, or at least what passes as human. Men like Jerome Senegal and Maurice Gaspard.''

"What do you know about Maurice Gaspard?'' she asked.

"That he's a rotten scumbag who enlists underage runaways to make him the richest pimp in town. And that if you cross him, you don't live to tell about it."

"You talk like a cop."

"I told you, I've spent the last two months prowling the city trying to find out what happened to Lily."

"Did you talk to the cops?"

"I filed a missing persons report. The cops don't worry a lot about runaways. Some of them don't worry much about Gaspard, either. Not that it matters all that much. If they arrest him, the D.A.'s office will probably lose the evidence and let him walk."

So he'd heard about Tony. "Bad news travels fast."

"Not bad news for Tony Arsenault. He's probably out there manufacturing more drugs and targeting some new victims in his spare time."

She swallowed hard, knowing he was right and somehow feeling responsible even though she was certain she'd returned the evidence to the file and locked the cabinet.

"Tell me about Sebastion Primeaux, Georgette."

"He's an exceptional attorney, very bright, super organized."

"And sleeping with Jerome Senegal and his band of thugs?"

"No. Absolutely not."

Tanner didn't argue the point, but his sharp intake of breath made it clear he didn't share her opinion. Tanner might be right about Gaspard, but not Sebastion. The man had his faults, but surely he wasn't involved with the mafia.

Yet if he were, it would explain a lot of things. Like how he could afford his lifestyle on a D.A.'s salary. Like his disposition that seemed to have taken a dramatic turn for the worse over the past six months or so. And like the missing evidence.

But there had to be other explanations. Sebastion was tough on crime. That's what got him elected, and what he preached to his staff continuously.

She took a deep breath and forced her thoughts back to Lily. If she was going to be out here keeping company with swamp creatures, she should be trying to conjure up the psychic connection.

"Was Lily born in New Orleans?" she asked, after a few minutes of concentrated but fruitless effort.

"No. We were in D.C. then, but we were living in New Orleans when Juliana finally decided she'd had enough and demanded a divorce."

"Had enough of what?"

"Of me. What else?"

"You don't seem that bad."

"Wait until you get to know me better."

For all her psychic powers, Georgette couldn't get a handle on Tanner Harrison. There were cops who didn't know as much about Jerome Senegal and Maurice Gaspard as he did. He'd lost touch with his daughter, yet he was obsessed with finding her. He was virile and masculine, yet he didn't try to act macho. Mainly he was a man on a mission and he wasn't going to let anything stand in his way.

It was a good half hour later when he pulled the oars inside the boat and let them drift. "This is getting us nowhere. Is there anything else we can try, anything at all?"

"Sometimes touch helps."

"Touch?" He reached across the boat and took her hands in his. "Like this."

A disturbing awareness zinged along her nerve endings, and this time she was almost certain the feelings had nothing to do with Lily. She forced her mind to concentrate on Lily.

Who are you with, Lily? Is he helping you or is he the enemy? Speak to me. Tell me you're alive. Tell me how to find you.

But the images had retreated and wherever they'd gone, she couldn't reach them. "It's no use, Tanner."

"I don't understand this gift of yours," he said, still holding her hands.

"I'm not sure anyone does."

"Who knows that you have it?"

"My mother...and you."

"That's all?"

"Yes." Admitting that seemed to make her far too vulnerable. She pulled away. "Let's go back to the cabin, Tanner. Please."

"Okay."

There had been no visions on their trip down the bayou, but the bonds that drew them together had grown stronger. It was as if the psychic powers that were forcing them to be together were also making them connect in an intimate, sensual way.

Or maybe she was just falling for the guy and looking for excuses. Either way she'd have to be careful that the attraction didn't go too far. No man wanted a psychic on a permanent basis. She'd come to terms with that long ago.

She was emotionally drained, tired and hungry by the time they reached the cabin, and was glad she hadn't thrown the rest of her chicken salad out after she'd only picked at it.

Tanner stepped out of the boat, tied it to the stake

and offered a hand to steady her as she stepped out of the boat.

"Wait."

"Is something wrong?"

"Yes." The word caught in her throat. This was crazy, crazier even than the visions and the way she felt drawn to Tanner. She stepped to the boggy bank. "I'm afraid, but I don't know why."

He pulled her into his arms just as the crack of gunfire echoed through the still, dark night.

Chapter Seven

Tanner shoved Georgette to the ground as the bullet hit a tree and sent fragments of bark flying like missiles. He fell on top of her, shielding her from whatever came next.

"Someone shot at us."

"You catch on fast," he whispered, hoping she wouldn't panic and start yelling.

"What do we do?"

"Keep quiet. Crawl behind that cluster of palmettos and stay low." He crawled behind her, keeping her moving until they were about three yards from where the bullet had hit. The dampness soaked through at his knees and elbows, and he had to flick a couple of crawling bugs off Georgette, fortunately before she realized they were there.

"Maybe it's your friend," she whispered once they'd stopped moving. "He may have come out here and thought we were trespassers."

"Walter would be way more likely to invite trespassers in for a beer than to shoot at them."

The shot didn't surprise him. He'd half expected something like this for weeks. He just hadn't expected it out here. Whoever had followed them had done a great job of avoiding detection. They weren't dealing with an amateur, which made this all the more dangerous. Rotten timing for Georgette to be caught with him.

Tanner listened for footfalls or a rustling in the grass around them. Nothing. Apparently the man was waiting for them to move, which meant he probably wasn't wearing night vision goggles.

He laid a hand on Georgette's shoulder and put his mouth close to her ear. "Stay here, and don't move unless I yell for you to get out of here. If I do, get back in the pirogue and row for all you're worth."

"I'm not going off in that boat in the dark."

"It's a lot safer than taking off through the swamp. Here," he said, handing her the flashlight. "You keep this."

She grabbed hold of his arm. "Where are you going?"

"To find our sniper."

"You can't do that. He'll kill you."

"Thanks for that vote of confidence."

"I think we should try to talk to him and see what he wants. I'm with the D.A.'s office, I can offer him…"

"Don't even think about it."

"But…"

"No buts." Attorneys. They thought they could talk their way out of anything. He retrieved a pistol holstered beneath his pants leg. He was traveling light tonight; his .38 was in the car.

"You have a gun?"

"Yeah, and I'm a crack shot. So stay put. And don't worry. I know what I'm doing."

Of course, his assailant probably did, too, but he

wouldn't point that out to Georgette. He kept to the bushes, working his way slowly toward the house. They'd left the kitchen light on and rectangles of light spread into the yard and offered scattered illumination around the back porch and steep steps.

There was no sign of the shooter, which meant he'd either retreated or was still hiding in the bushes near the house waiting for them to move. Tanner had never been a patient guy. He stooped and picked up a limb that had fallen from a nearby willow tree.

He tossed it toward the back steps, then watched for the flash from a firing gun. The sniper didn't disappoint him. He shot off a round of bullets before he realized that the movement at the back steps wasn't Tanner.

Tanner returned the fire, then heard the crushing stamp of the sniper's feet as he took off through the bushes, heading around the side of the house.

Tanner moved slower, staying out of sight, his finger on the trigger and ready to shoot. By the time he rounded the corner of the house, he could hear a car engine revving to life. The guy took off without turning on his lights, but Tanner fired off a quick round in the direction of the noise.

From the sound, at least one of the bullets hit the car. Tanner yanked the keys from his pocket and jumped in his car. He shoved the key into the ignition and turned it, but the damn engine didn't even sputter.

No way that was by chance. The guy had yanked a few wires—or worse. He'd meant business, and if his bullet had been a couple of inches closer, he'd have accomplished what he came for. Tanner would be lying in the swamp with a bullet in his head.

Or if he'd missed the other way, it might be Georgette lying dead. Sonofabitch. He'd practically forced her to help him then dragged her into danger.

He got out of the car and slammed the door behind him. There was movement at the side of the house. Georgette, peeking from behind a fan of palmetto fronds and framed in light filtering from the house. If he'd been the sniper, she'd have been an easy target.

"Thanks for staying put," he called.

Georgette lifted the flashlight and aimed the beam at his face. "You didn't call for me. I thought you might be shot and bleeding to death."

"In which case you should be in the pirogue getting the hell out of here."

She crossed the few steps between them and slipped into his arms. The move surprised him, yet he held her close and buried his face in her thick shiny hair. Only now, the dark strands were streaked with mud from having been thrown to the ground.

She was trembling. He was a little shaky himself, but not from the gunfire or even the close call. He'd had too many of those over the years. They gave him a quick burst of adrenaline. Other than that they were more like a summer thunderstorm, inconvenient and annoying, but not nerve-shattering.

Holding a woman like Georgette Delacroix in his arms was a different matter. She was too soft, too smart, too desirable. And even thinking these things scared the hell out of him.

"Can we get out of here now?" she asked, finally pulling from his arms.

"We can if I can get the car started. Our sniper buddy apparently did a little mechanical work while we were cruising the bayou."

She groaned, but didn't fall back into his arms.

"You work for a transport company. Call someone and get us transported back to town."

"I will, if I have to. Why don't you wait inside while I check out the damage to the car."

"You'll need me to hold the flashlight for you while you look at the engine."

"I have a trouble light in the trunk. It fits right on my head and gives me all the light I need." Besides he didn't want her around while he called Conrad Burke and reported the situation. The Confidential agents were on their own in the field, but Burke liked to know when violence came into play.

He waited until she was inside, then dialed Burke's number, trying to think how he was going to explain being at a fishing camp south of Morgan City with one of the junior prosecutors from the D.A.'s office when he couldn't tell Burke about the psychic visions. He'd known he'd have problems when he'd made that promise, but then Georgette hadn't given him any alternative.

He'd never lied to his boss before. He hated doing it now. His life was growing more complicated by the minute, but still it couldn't begin to compare with what Lily must be going through. And he'd lie or bargain with the devil himself before he'd let anything get in the way of finding her.

He punched in Burke's number, and waited for him to answer. It was eight long rings before he did.

"Hello."

"I hate to bother you at home."

"Don't worry, Harrison. Your timing was great. I just finished changing one dirty diaper and was about to start the next. Marilyn took over for me when she saw the call was from you."

"Don't tell me twins even poop at the same time?"

"Not always. What's up?"

"I had a little fun of my own tonight. Someone just took a shot at me, actually several shots."

"I'm assuming he missed."

"By inches." Tanner covered the basics, omitting the fact that he was with someone from Sebastion Primeaux's office.

"Do you have any idea who fired the shots?"

"My first guess would be someone Gaspard sent to stop me from asking questions about Lily."

"Did you get a look at the car?"

"No. It's pitch-dark out here."

"Keep me posted. In the meantime I have a little news for you, too, unless you've already heard from your partner."

"Not since the meeting this afternoon."

"Bartley was snooping around Tony Arsenault's apartment tonight when he saw this sexy dame dressed to kill get out of a taxi and pay The Knife a visit. Bartley figured it was one of Gaspard's working girls, so he stuck around and followed her taxi back into town."

"Where'd she go?"

"To an apartment over a shop on Royal Street. Several more ladies arrived along with a dozen or more older, well-dressed men. He recognized one of them."

"Anyone I know?"

"You've probably heard of him. Paul Haversack. He ran for governor a few years back, but lost."

"Closing down Gaspard's so-called club didn't slow the operation down long."

"I turned the information over to the chief of police. That's his game now, and I think we should leave this in his ballpark unless he can't handle it. In the meantime, I thought you might like to know where you can find Gaspard."

"I appreciate that."

"Watch your back, Tanner. I know how badly you want to find Lily, but you won't do her any good if you're six feet under."

"I know." The anger and desperation hit again, swirling inside him at gale force. He couldn't think of Gaspard without getting this overwhelming urge to beat his head in until it looked like a smashed pumpkin.

But he couldn't help Lily from a jail cell, either. He finished the call and checked out the car. The battery wires were loose. He reattached the wires and started the car. It purred like a kitten.

Georgette was waiting for him when he walked inside. Her face was scrubbed clean of the mud and the makeup. She looked younger, innocent, nothing like an attorney. For one stupid second he imagined what her lips would taste like. His body reacted so swiftly, he had to turn away to keep her from noticing. All the wrong feelings at the worst possible time. And for the wrong woman.

Georgette had everything going for her. Young. Attractive. Smart. A brilliant career in front of her. No reason at all for her to get mixed up with a man who'd never once got a relationship right.

But when he turned back and looked into her dark, mesmerizing eyes, he knew it was a good thing they were not spending the night together.

"I'D LIKE to see you to your door," Tanner said, when he rounded the corner of Julia Street and neared the condo complex.

"That's not necessary. There's a security guard at the door. The building is very safe."

He'd still feel better if he knew that whoever had attacked them tonight hadn't decided to extend his murderous intent to Georgette. "Humor me," he said. "I'm a hardheaded guy."

"Suit yourself. There's a parking garage."

"Is it security controlled as well?"

"It's monitored by surveillance cameras and residents have a code to open the full-gated door."

Everything they needed to keep honest people or maybe even common criminals out. Senegal's hit men could undoubtedly find a way around the security devices. He followed her directions to the gate.

"I don't have my opener with me, so you'll have to punch in the code," she said.

She gave him the six-digit code, and he committed it to memory. Her parking space was on the second level, not far from the elevator. He checked out the surveillance setup. Everything seemed in order, including the small light that indicated the cameras nearest them were operating.

Her condo was on the sixth floor, river side. "You must have a great view."

"If that's a request for a nightcap, the answer is no. I've had more than enough excitement for one night."

"I'm flattered that you think a nightcap with me would be exciting, but I wasn't thinking of having a drink. I would like to stay while you take a look around and make sure everything's okay."

Tiny furrows lined her brow. "Why wouldn't it be?"

"Just a precaution."

She rummaged for her key, but instead of opening the door, she leaned against it and faced him. "Tell me what's going on, Tanner."

"You know as much as I do. You were there when we were shot at."

"But I don't know all there is to know about you."

"I drive a delivery truck."

"You carry a concealed weapon. And I saw you check out the surveillance cameras. You act more like a cop than a truck driver."

"I'm just a worried father," he lied, though that seemed the most accurate description of what he was right now.

He couldn't tell her about his connection with New Orleans Confidential, not when she worked for one of the men they were investigating. But then he couldn't have told her even if she was just a psychic helping him locate Lily.

"I won't go in if that makes you uneasy. You just unlock the door and take a look around. I don't expect there to be anything amiss. I'm just a cautious kind of guy, especially when some crackpot fires a shot at me."

"Okay." She went inside and was back minutes later.

"Everything's fine."

"Good."

"Good night, Tanner, and I'm sorry about the visions. I really hoped I could help."

"I'm not giving up. I'll call you tomorrow. And in the meantime, take my cell-phone number." He wrote it down on the back of a business card and handed it to her.

The night was over. It was time to go, yet they both stood there until the moment grew tense with a sizzling awareness that wouldn't quit.

He leaned in closer, aching to kiss her good-night. Knowing he shouldn't. Finally she saved them.

"Talk to you tomorrow, Tanner. Take care of yourself." And then she closed the door.

TANNER HARRISON was more than a worried father.

That thought stayed with Georgette as she slipped out of her shoes and headed for the shower to rid her body of the dirt, perspiration and smell of the swamp. Even after spending the evening with Tanner and facing a sniper, she couldn't figure him out.

He wasn't out to hurt her. If he were, he'd had the perfect chance tonight, but still he was pulling her into a dangerous game where she didn't know the rules or the players.

If he'd contacted her first, she'd be almost certain she was a pawn. But it was the dreaded gift that had not only brought them together but linked them together so intricately that she couldn't break the connection without affecting the fate of his daughter.

The very thing she'd fought all her life was happening. Her life was being controlled by psychic powers. And by a man who both intrigued and frightened her.

She had no choice now but to use every means available to investigate his past while praying the gift would lead her to Lily before it was too late.

Unless it was too late already.

She stepped under the hot spray praying for the images and hating the gift and its volatile ways more than ever.

TANNER STOOD outside the Bourbon Street apartment where Maurice Gaspard was entertaining and pulling in the bucks with the help of his underage prostitutes. The entryway was a street-level door crowded between two storefronts. A brawny bouncer wearing a pair of jeans and a muscle shirt stood outside the door, leering at a group of college-aged girls in the Quarter for a night of fun.

There was no way Tanner could bully his way by the giant thug, but there were ways around that. Tanner waited until the street was crowded, then waded into the midst of the tightest group.

"Hey, somebody just lifted my wallet," he yelled, stumbling backward as if he were intoxicated.

The crowd movement came to a grinding halt as everyone checked their pockets for their own money and looked around to see who was guilty. A college guy bumped into an older man and spilled his beer down the guy's neck. The old guy yelled an obscenity. Somebody pushed someone and a fight broke out.

More than Tanner had hoped for, but just what he needed. Cops seemed to materialize from the overhanging cloud of humidity and the bouncer took a few steps into the street to get a better look at the chaos.

Tanner disappeared in the crowd and slipped through the door unnoticed. Once inside, he had no trouble finding the party. All he had to do was follow the music. No one looked up as he joined the celebration.

The men were all older, just as Bartley had reported. The women were all young and beautiful, or at least classy and sexily clad. Tanner wondered how many of the men were either being introduced to or were already addicted to Category Five, the sex-enhancing, heart-rate-spiraling drug that had proved especially dangerous to older men with a heart condition.

Tanner spotted Gaspard on a balcony overlooking Bourbon Street talking to a black girl so young she looked as if she were playing dress-up in her mother's red cocktail dress and a pair of shoes so high-heeled she'd probably break a leg if she fell off them.

He threaded his way through the couples. "Nice party," he said, stepping out the open French doors and onto the balcony.

Gaspard turned, and Tanner watched his satisfied smile settle into a strained frown.

"Go back inside, Becky. I need to talk to our *uninvited* guest."

The girl stared at Tanner as if she were sizing him up before she walked away. Tanner's heart plunged to his shoes. He was looking at the girl in red, but he saw Lily. Sizing up men. Planning to seduce them for money. His little girl.

Tanner fought the urge to pick Gaspard up and toss him over the railing to be crushed on the street below.

"This is a private party, Tanner."

"So you know who I am?"

"Everyone knows who you are. You're a trouble-maker."

"Where is Lily Harrison?"

"I don't know anyone by that name."

"You're lying. I know my daughter worked for you."

"That's possible. I used to hire waitresses and a few dancers for a club I operated. I don't remember all their names."

"She was only seventeen, Gaspard. And you hired her to do more than dance or serve drinks."

"Are you intimating that your daughter is a whore, Tanner?"

Tanner clutched the balcony railing to keep from wrapping his hands around Gaspard's neck. "I'm asking if you know where she is."

"Then you have your answer. I don't recall ever having met a Lily Harrison. Now I'm afraid I'll have to ask you to leave. As I said, this is a private party."

"Your party looks an awful lot like the kind of underage prostitution ring that got the McDonough Club shut down. You were just clever enough to disappear into thin air when the raid went down."

"Well, here I am, a free man, attending parties and living the good life. Ain't America a great country?"

Tanner stuck his face in Gaspard's, backing him up against the railing. "You'll rot in jail before this is over, unless I find out you've hurt Lily. In that case, you'll never live to see another jail cell."

"Are you threatening me?"

"I'd call it making you a promise."

Tanner turned away and strode from the room before he forgot he was one of the good guys and took that stinking slimeball out right here in front of his *guests.*

The bouncer was still waiting at the door when Tanner left. "If I were you, I'd look for a new job," Tanner said. "Your boss is hot as Hades that you let me in, and you know how vicious Gaspard gets when he's mad.''

Tanner didn't wait around to see if the guy heeded his warning.

GASPARD STOOD on the balcony, watching the revelry taking place on Bourbon Street while he considered what to do about Tanner Harrison.

Lily was one of the red-hot firecrackers. She should have been eliminated and would have been if her father had been anyone but Tanner Harrison, ex-CIA, currently, who knew what. Senegal figured he might even be undercover CIA or FBI.

So now Lily was one of Senegal's pawns and Tanner was a loose cannon who needed to be eliminated. Only, Senegal couldn't know that Gaspard was behind the hit.

He gave it some more thought, then took out his phone and made a call to a couple of guys who could handle what he needed and would keep their mouths shut. All they'd want in return was a little action on the side. Gaspard had a roomful of ladies who could handle the action.

TANNER CUT THROUGH Pirates Alley then walked past St. Louis Cathedral and Jackson Square. He dropped a dollar in the hat of a sax player blowing out a familiar version of ''When the Saints Go Marching In,'' but didn't give a second look to the mimic covered in gold paint standing on the corner like a misplaced statue.

It was nearing midnight, the witching hour for the Quarter when the partying tourists crossed paths with the late-night locals who never really got started until

the early-morning hours. He stopped for a beer in a
to-go cup, then kept walking with no particular des-
tination in mind.

Are you intimating your daughter is a whore?

The words clamored in his head. He'd wanted to
kill Gaspard for uttering them, but it was truth that
hurt so much. And the anger. Not at Lily. He could
never be angry at Lily. She'd been the sweetest kid
in the world. Always ready with a hug and a smile.

She'd written him a poem for Father's Day, the first
one they hadn't spent together. She'd been eight, ad-
justing to life in London. He'd been thirty-four, missing her so much he'd hardly been able to stand it.

He'd carried the poem around in his pocket until
the paper was yellowed and torn. Then he'd put it
away for safekeeping before it completely disinte-
grated. But he remembered it, word for word.

No matter how far I am from you,

Something moved behind Tanner and he snapped
to attention, realizing he'd wound up on a deserted
street. Instinctively, he went for his gun and moved
against the side of a brick building.

Too late. Pain ripped through his body and streams
of blood poured down the back of his neck. He tried
to focus as a fist slammed into his face, but the world
was spinning in a black haze. He collapsed to the
broken concrete sidewalk. The last thing he remembered was a heel kicking into his stomach.

And the thought that just like the victim he'd found
in the Quarter a few nights ago, he was going to die.

Chapter Eight

Tanner came to and turned away from the glare of a bright flashlight shining directly in his eyes. Strange voices that sounded as if they were being filtered through water clamored for his attention. He blinked, saw swirling shapes, then closed his eyes again and tried to roll away from the light. Pain shot through every muscle, and with it the memory of the beating.

He didn't know much else, but he was certain he was alive. Death couldn't possibly hurt this much. The voices became clearer.

"Somebody beat the crap out of him."

"We should call an ambulance, or the police."

"I don't want to get involved in a police investigation. We've got a plane to catch in a few hours."

"We can't just leave him like this."

"If it gets back to my wife or your husband that we're out partying together this time of night, we'll be dead. Definitely be the last convention she ever lets me attend without her."

"They'll never find out."

"Until the New Orleans cops start calling you at home to ask more questions."

"It doesn't seem right to leave him like this."

"Someone else will come along. Let's get out of here."

The light went out of his face. When he opened his eyes, he was alone. He lay there for a while longer, then managed to sit and finally to stand using the brick exterior of the building as support. It took a few minutes longer to remember where his car was parked. Two blocks away. He'd never make it.

He started to crumble back to the sidewalk, then thought of Lily and found the will to keep standing. If he didn't stay alive, there would be no one to find her and bring her home.

He stumbled along. A car passed but didn't slow down. He probably looked like just another drunk staggering home in the wee hours of the morning. Finally, he came to his car, crawled inside, locked the door and passed out again.

The next time he opened his eyes, the black of night had lightened to a dingy gray. A garbage truck rumbled by and the clatter of banging trash cans sent his head into orbit. He rummaged in his pockets for the keys, found them and started the engine.

He pulled from the curb and checked his phone messages, as always hoping there was something from Lily. But it was a man's voice that rang in his ears.

"That was only a warning. Stay away from Georgette, or next time you'll both end up dead."

He groaned and turned onto Rampart, dread mixing with the pain. This had nothing to do with Georgette, and if those bastards had done anything to her, he'd...

His mind flicked on and off like the blinking light at the corner. He had to check on Georgette and make sure she was all right.

Somehow the code flashed across his brain when he stopped at the entrance to her parking garage. He punched it in, then drove through, wincing as the gate clanged shut behind him. Sixth floor. Condo on the river side facing Algiers. He dragged himself from the car, then remembered the .38. Painfully he reached back, unlocked the glove compartment and retrieved his weapon of choice.

His head was pounding when he reached the elevator, and the bell sounded like a gong. He pushed the six and leaned against the wall, conscious only of the weight of the gun in his right hand.

And that he had to make it to Georgette's door.

GEORGETTE WOKE SUDDENLY, afraid, but not sure why. She lay very still and listened to the quiet sound of her own breathing. A few seconds later, she heard two loud knocks, and her heart skipped a beat before jumping into a frantic pattern.

No one should be at her door. The building was secure. She'd made certain of that before she bought the condo. A woman who prosecuted criminals made enemies of the worst of humanity.

But there it was again, softer this time. She grabbed her cell phone from the bedside table, then slid her feet out from the tangle of sheets to the floor. She'd look out the peephole and if there was anyone there except the security guard, she'd call 911.

She peered into the hallway. She didn't see anyone, but she heard a shuffle of feet. Someone was definitely out there. She'd already dialed a nine and a one when Tanner moved into her line of vision.

Her hands trembled as she loosened the safety

latch, opened the door and pulled a bloody, bruised and swollen Tanner inside.

"You okay?" he mumbled.

"Yes, but you're not!" she cried.

"I'm not great." To prove his point, he clutched his stomach and swayed against her.

"What happened? Who did this to you?" Her heart pounded wildly in her chest.

"A rebel army I hope. I'd hate to think one or two guys put this much hurt on me."

"What are you doing here? You should be in a hospital."

"Nah. I hate those places. They're full of sick people."

She helped him to the couch, holding onto him as he dropped to it and let his head fall back on the cushions.

She took the gun from his hand and deposited it on the mantle and out of sight. Guns always made her nervous. "Where were you when you were attacked?"

"In the Quarter."

"This time of the morning?"

"No. Earlier. They caught me from behind. Never saw them coming—or leaving."

"You need X-rays, Tanner, to make sure nothing's broken and you need to be checked for internal injuries."

She knew her voice was betraying her deep concern for Tanner, but she couldn't help it; he mattered to her.

"Naw. I'm fine. Just sore and a little woozy."

"And bloody. You have a cut on the back of your

head and your right eye is swollen closed. Lie still. I'll get a wet cloth and some peroxide.''

He put his hand to the cut. ''Just a scratch. It's already quit bleeding.''

She examined the wound. It actually wasn't that deep, but blood was matted in his hair and there was a goose egg on the back of his head that could use an ice pack.

''How did you get in the building?''

''Drove in. Used your code.''

''You're in no condition to drive.'' More to the point, he should be in a hospital instead of on her couch, but she wouldn't push the issue yet. Better to keep him calm and administer some emergency first aid. Unless he blacked out on her. The second he did that, she was calling for an ambulance.

Her nerves managed to survive until she collected an ice pack, a pan of cool water, some towels, a bottle of peroxide and some spray antiseptic. She sat them all on the coffee table within easy reach, while she helped him out of his torn and bloody shirt.

She dipped a cloth in the cool water, wrung it out and dabbed gingerly at the blood that clung to his hair and the right side of his head. He grimaced, but didn't complain. Once the wound was as clean as she could get it without pressure, she sprayed it with antiseptic. ''I still think you should see a doctor.''

''Would ruin a perfectly good Sunday. Besides, we've got business to take care of today, and with luck, your psychic powers are going to show up for work.''

''You should rest a bit first.'' She applied an ice pack to his black eye and swollen cheek and another to the lump on the back of his head. That done, she untied his shoes and he kicked out of them, albeit slowly. She lifted his stockinged feet to the sofa. At least she tried to. They hung over the end.

"You can have my bed," she said. "I'm wide-awake now anyway."

"We can share. You'd be safe enough since I can barely move."

Safe from him, but not from her imagination. He hobbled to the bed, this time without her assistance. Even in the half hour or so he'd been in her condo, he'd gotten steadier on his feet. She jerked the top sheet back and he settled into the same spot she'd climbed out of when he'd knocked on her door.

She plumped the pillows for him, then backed away. His long frame was outlined against the crisp white sheets. Even hurt, he was an undeniable hunk of a guy. His face was badly misshapen from the swelling, but his thick brown hair, still damp from the sponge bath, fell over his slightly crooked eyebrows, reminding her how devilishly handsome he really was.

And he was in her bed. So, before she changed her mind, she crawled between the sheets and settled in beside him. She was sure she'd lost her mind, but not sure it made a hell of a lot of difference in a world where people took potshots at her in the swamp and a man like Tanner got beaten to a pulp just because he wanted to find his daughter.

THE LOUD, ANGRY VOICES erupted in Georgette's head, the language so profane it turned her stomach. The room they were in was small and bare except for a couple of rockers and a table that looked homemade. It was unbearably hot, the air heavy and pungent with the smell of garlic and fish.

"You get out now, or I'll kill you and feed you to my dog."

"Crazy Eugene. That's a good name for you, you crazy Cajun. You want to die for some British slut?"

Blood flew across the room. It was in Georgette's face, on her clothes, dripping from her hands.

...her blood will be on your hands.

No, please... It wasn't Lily's blood. Or was it? She couldn't tell anymore. But it was red and sticky and it just kept coming. Georgette reached for Lily. If she could touch her she could pull her free of the nightmare, but when Georgette clamped her hand about Lily's arm, the girl's flesh turned to blood. Georgette shrank away, and slowly, the room, the men and even the blood got caught up in a whirlwind and blown away.

Georgette sat up in bed, spinning in the nightmare for interminably long seconds before reality took hold. She eased out of bed, careful not to wake Tanner. His breathing was steady and strong, the only reassuring thing in her life right now.

Tiptoeing to her desk, she pulled out a pen and paper and printed the words *Crazy Eugene*. It wasn't much to go on, but it was more than they'd had before.

Crazy Eugene. A Cajun man. Likely living in the swamp where Lily had been on the run. He was the name they needed. Georgette took her phone to the kitchen, started a pot of coffee, then made a call to the state police office in Baton Rouge. There was always a chance they'd heard of him, especially if he had a criminal record.

She went through three clerks and realized Saturday morning was not the best time to seek information. After the third clerk, she was put through to a patrolman in the Lafayette area who said he'd never had any dealing with a Crazy Eugene, but he'd ask around and also pose her question on the statewide information bulletin that went out daily. He also did a quick check that only ascertained that the man was not currently on anyone's wanted list.

She poured her coffee and took it out on the balcony. A cruise ship was docked at the Riverwalk Market Place, and a stream of people was disembarking. A ferry was churning the water on its trip from Algiers to the Spanish Plaza at the foot of Canal Street. And just beyond the ferry, a tug pushed a huge barge down the middle of the busy, muddy Mississippi River. Business as usual, but not for her or Tanner—and not for Lily.

"Nice view. Prosecutors in the D.A.'s office live well."

She jumped at Tanner's voice, then turned to find him leaning against the French door she'd left open.

"Mortgaged to the hilt," she said, walking over to take a closer look at his wound and the black eye in the sunshine. "But I like it." She fit her fingers over the bump on the back of his head. "Swelling's gone down some. How do you feel?"

"Like I wrestled a couple of twelve-foot 'gators and lost."

"You look a lot like that, too."

"I figure I'm lucky to be alive."

"Do you think they left you for dead?"

"More likely someone showed up before they were finished and scared them off."

"Did you get a look at your attackers?"

"No. They came at me from behind." He rubbed the spot on the back of his head and winced as if remembering the initial slam. "I'm sure they were some of Gaspard's maggots since I'd just made a surprise guest appearance at one of his fornicating frolics."

"Where was that?"

"Third floor over a souvenir shop on Bourbon Street. Someone tipped me off where to find him."

She listened to his account of the meeting, more amazed than ever that he was alive. Maurice Gaspard didn't hesitate to use violence. The recent deaths of so many of his prostitutes was proof of that, and she lived for the day she could obtain enough evidence to take him to trial for even one of those murders.

She prayed it wouldn't be for Lily's.

"I had another vision this morning, Tanner."

His eyes registered his interest. "Lily?"

"Yes. This time there were two men." She detailed the vision, seeing the blood as vividly as she had this morning while in the throes of the trance.

"Crazy Eugene." Tanner repeated the name, spitting it out as if it left a bitter taste on his tongue.

"Do you know him?"

"I know of him."

"How?"

He shook his head, but didn't answer. More of his secrets. For a truck driver, he had a lot of them.

"Mind if I take a quick shower here? I want to get on my way."

"On your way where?"

"To find Crazy Eugene and perhaps my daughter."

"You know where he lives?"

"Somewhere around Beau Bridge."

"You're in no shape to go looking for him. Call the cops, or the state police. This is their job."

"It's not a job we're talking about. It's Lily."

There was no use arguing with him, so there was only one thing to do. "I'm going with you, Tanner."

"No place for a woman."

"Then think of me as a pushy attorney who won't take no for an answer. Besides, if we get there and Lily's not there, I may be the only one who can help you find her."

"WHY ARE YOU stopping here?" Georgette asked when Tanner pulled into the back parking lot of Crescent City Transports.

"I just have to pick something up. Hope you don't mind waiting in the car. I'll only be a few minutes."

"I'll wait."

Good, since there was no way he could get her past the Confidential security check. Admittance was by eye scan only. Tanner took the elevator to his office and pulled up the computer file on Crazy Eugene Boudreaux. His name had been one of the ones that had come up when the Confidential agency first started looking at known criminal elements in the south Louisiana area.

They'd excluded him from the investigation into the drug and underage prostitution problems in New Orleans and also from their quest to find out why the small band of rebels from Nilia was in the Big Easy.

He studied the file, making mental notes of the facts and hard-copy notes of the location listed as his home address.

Eugene had never been part of the mob. At least

that was what the records indicated. But he had been in and out of jail all his life, the last time for murdering a guy he'd argued with in a bar in Beau Bridge.

Eugene had gotten off on the grounds of being mentally incompetent to stand trial due to a severe psychological disorder that had gone untreated. He was placed in a state mental hospital. A year later some shrink had said they'd done all they could for him and sent him home.

Tanner would have loved to call one of the other Confidential agents for backup—anyone but Mason Bartley. But there was no way to explain any of this and keep Georgette's psychic powers a secret.

He didn't like it that she was going along, but he'd have had to tie her to the bedpost to leave her behind and that hadn't seemed like a particularly good idea, considering she was a damn pushy prosecuting attorney who was his only real lead to Lily.

The other feelings he had about Georgette were too confusing to deal with. Not the attraction. That was a given. She was a very exotic and beautiful woman. Dark hair, dark eyes, luscious breasts.

But pretty women were a dime a dozen in New Orleans. It was the way she was getting inside him that frightened him. In his forty-three years of living, he'd only let one woman do that, and Juliana had all but destroyed him. He was not going there again.

Satisfied that he had all the info available on Crazy Eugene, he flicked off the computer and grabbed a blue T-shirt from the hall closet, one emblazoned in bold black letters across the front with the words Crescent City Transports. He yanked off his blood-stained shirt and pushed his arms and head through the replacement.

And once more he was off, this time visiting a crazy murderer who lived in the Atchafalaya Basin.

JEROME SENEGAL left early mass and started walking toward Lafayette Park. He didn't trust offices or automobiles for meetings that mattered. They were far too easy to bug, especially with the authorities crawling all over him these days.

And this was a very important meeting.

Senegal picked up his pace. Ricardo Gonzalez was to meet him at the park in ten minutes, and the rebel ringleader was never late.

He spun around at the sound of approaching footsteps, his hand moving instinctively to the holster under his lightweight suit jacket.

"I thought that was you, Mr. Senegal, though I couldn't be sure from the back."

"Are you following me, Bartley?"

"I just wanted to say hello."

"I thought you were in jail for some cheap con job you screwed up in Shreveport."

"Can't keep a good man down. You know that."

"So what are you up to these days?"

"Looking for work. Thought you might have some."

"I'm a businessman, Bartley. Why would I want to hire a guy who couldn't handle a simple swindle?"

"I made a little mistake, but that doesn't mean I'd make another one."

"What is it you want to do for me?"

"Whatever needs doing. I need some bucks, and I

need to get back in the action. I'm withering away trying to be a law-abiding citizen.''

Senegal glanced at his watch. ''Call me tomorrow. We'll set up an appointment.''

''Thanks. I really appreciate this, Senegal. Whatever you need. I'm your man.''

''Right now I need you to disappear. And don't tell anyone we've talked.''

''Not a soul. Believe me, I wouldn't tell a soul about that.''

Senegal entered the park and went to the bench in the back corner. He was a few minutes early, but Gonzalez was already there and wearing an arrogant smirk.

He hated the man with a passion. But this wasn't about friendship. It was a business deal and Senegal needed Gonzalez more than the pompous Nilian rebel needed him. He walked up beside him so they could talk quietly. Fortunately, there was no one else around.

''Tomorrow's the delivery date, Senegal. Are you making good on our deal?''

Senegal hated that he had to look up at the man to meet his gaze, but he did it. ''I've had a few problems.''

''A deal is a deal, man.'' Gonzalez flexed his muscles. ''You don't deliver. I don't deliver.''

''I'll deliver. I just need more time.''

''We're in the middle of a revolution in Nilia. Do you think I can go back and tell Black Death to put the war on hold while you pussyfoot around?''

Senegal felt the sweat pool under his armpits. He hated kowtowing to this Nilian thug with his scorpion tattoo and his slicked-back black hair, but he had to have the deal. "A few more days, Gonzalez. That's all I need."

"That's good because we've got a ship arriving in port early next week, could be as early as Tuesday, and we're sailing back to Nilia on that boat. If you don't deliver, your supply of drugs will go back with us. It's not personal, you understand. It's business."

"Of course, business."

"There is one little catch, Senegal. In our country, a broken deal means death."

Gonzalez spit out the threat, then turned and strode away.

Senegal told him what he could do with his country and his attitude, but he did it under his breath. A day or two more. That's all he had. Gonzalez was a crazed revolutionary, and Senegal knew from his reputation that he did not make idle threats.

He had to get two million more dollars from somewhere and he needed it now.

THE RUSTIC FISHING CAMP outside Morgan City they'd visited last night was a mansion compared to Crazy Eugene's home. It was basically a shack on the Atchafalaya River. The porch was rotting away and the place leaned so far to the left, it looked as if it might collapse at any second.

Georgette stayed close to Tanner and tried to avoid the soggiest ground, but her shoes still sank into the boggy earth with every step. A crow flew to a low branch of a cypress tree and cawed loudly as they approached the door.

"Do you think he's trying to tell us something?" Georgette asked.

"You're the psychic. What do you think?"

She left the question unanswered, mainly because she had a very uneasy feeling about this. The uneasiness changed to dread the closer they got to the shack. The crow cawed again and flew away. Smart bird.

Her foot was on the first rotting step when she saw the blood. It was seeping under the door and running onto the weathered porch.

The nightmare had become reality.

Chapter Nine

"Get back, Georgette. You don't want to see this."

"I'm a prosecuting attorney. I've seen..." She gagged at the sight and stumbled backward. Tanner was right. She did not want to see this.

One man had multiple stab wounds in his chest and abdomen, the other had a bullet through his brain. Her stomach lurched and she grabbed a few quick shallow breaths. "This explains the bloody visions I woke to this morning."

Tanner wrapped a steadying arm around her shoulder. "I know you're a thick-skinned attorney, but why don't you wait in the car?"

"By myself? With a killer around? No, thanks."

"The victims have been dead a few hours. I'm sure the killer's not hanging around. Lock the doors, and lay on the horn if you need me."

"I've seen the worst. I'll be okay." At least she hoped she'd seen the worst, and she had no intention of leaving Tanner's side until she was certain that Lily's body wasn't somewhere inside this shack.

"Careful not to touch or move anything," Tanner said, inching closer to the stabbing victim. "We don't want to dirty the crime scene."

She'd have been hesitant to touch anything in this place even if it hadn't been a crime scene. Not that she'd have been concerned about dirtying it. It couldn't have been cleaned this decade. Mud caked the floor, spiderwebs hung from the bare light fixtures, and a big, black cockroach had just crawled across the floor and disappeared under the stained couch.

The kitchen and living area were basically one room, and there were dishes with the leftovers of what appeared to be breakfast still sitting on a wooden table. Breakfast for two.

"I assume the non-Hispanic is Crazy Eugene," she said.

"Probably a good assumption." Tanner picked up a bent coat hanger from the floor, then stooped over the body of the man with the knife embedded in his chest. Sliding the hooked end of the hanger under the man's bloody shirt, he pulled the fabric away from the wounds. A large, menacing black scorpion was tattooed on the right side of the man's chest.

Tanner muttered a string of curses, then stood and tossed the hanger to the floor.

"What does the scorpion tattoo mean?"

"I don't know."

She didn't buy that, but she let it slide—for the time being. She followed Tanner and someone's bloody footprints to the open bathroom door.

"Looks like our killer was male," Tanner said, pointing to the footprints facing the toilet and the seat which had been left up. Georgette had never considered the alternative.

There was only one other door, a closed one in the left corner of the room, also with bloody footprints leading to it. Georgette stayed a step behind Tanner, stepping where he did and avoiding messing up the bloody prints. But this time she waited to get his reaction before she peered around him and into the room.

"No more bodies," he said, obviously relieved.

Assured of that, she walked into the small, sparsely furnished room. Some dirty clothes were piled in the corner next to a stack of yellowed newspapers. A cracked pottery bowl half filled with a brownish mixture that looked like soft mud and smelled of pungent herbs sat on a wooden plank table next to an unmade bed.

Tanner walked over to the table. "Appears to be a homemade poultice of some kind," he said, leaning close to take a whiff of the mud-like concoction. "And I'm guessing these strips of white cloth were used for bandages."

The sun poured through the one dingy window, highlighting the dust that danced in the air and layered the table. Something silvery glimmered from the floor at the edge of the bed.

Forgetting the warning about not touching anything, Georgette stooped and picked up what turned out to be a delicate chain with a dangling silver heart.

"I doubt this belonged to Eugene," she said, holding up the necklace for Tanner to see. He took it from her hand and turned the heart over to study the inscription. She leaned in close so that she could read it as well.

Love always, Dad.

"This is Lily's necklace," he said gruffly. "I sent it to her for her last birthday."

"Then she was here," Georgette said.

"Yeah. Damn. If we'd only gotten here sooner…"

"Where do you think she is now?" Stupid question, Georgette decided, one second after she'd blurted it out. If Lily wasn't here, she was most likely with the madman who'd committed the brutal double murder.

Tanner slipped the necklace into his pocket. "I want to take a look around outside." He backed out of the room, slowly, as if committing everything about it to memory.

Georgette held her nose and averted her gaze from the bodies as they walked past them again and out the door. Tanner spent the next half hour combing the swampy area around the house, poking and foraging around every bush. If his injuries from last night's beating slowed him down, she couldn't tell it. His concerns for his daughter apparently overrode pain.

"Do you think Lily could be hiding out in the swamp?"

"I haven't found any tracks, not even subtle ones, which leads me to believe she left in a vehicle. There were fresh tire prints beside ours when we parked."

She hadn't noticed that. It amazed her that Tanner had. But then he'd noticed lots of details about the crime scene. And he'd known to look for the scorpion. None of which added up to just a truck-driving father and that fact was making her increasingly anxious.

"We have to report this to the authorities, Tanner."

"And how are you going to explain that we happened to be here?"

Drat! She hadn't thought of that. She definitely couldn't tell them she'd fallen into a trance and seen

Crazy Eugene and an eruption õf blood. They'd never buy it anyway. Still...

"I work for the D.A.'s office," she said, "I can't just ignore two murders."

"I don't want the local cop crew out here just yet."

Her concerns swelled to choking suspicions. "I may be gullible to a point, Tanner, but we've passed that point. You know too much about people like Crazy Eugene, Maurice Gaspard, Jerome Senegal and men with scorpion tattoos. And you handled the crime scene like a cop. Level with me. Who are you and what are you involved in?"

Tanner stared into the swamp. The tendons in his neck were stretched taut, his back straight, his jaw clenched. Finally he turned to face her, his gaze so intense, she felt as if his soul were reaching from it and touching hers.

"It's a complicated story, Georgette."

"I don't doubt it, but if you want my help in finding Lily, I have to know what you're involved in."

He took a deep breath and exhaled slowly. "Okay. I guess there's no getting around this."

"No."

"The other day you made me promise that I wouldn't tell anyone of your psychic powers. I did as you asked. Now I have to ask that same promise of you. You can't repeat to anyone what I'm about to tell you."

"I can't keep information a secret if it links you to something criminal."

"It doesn't. Do you swear that you won't tell a soul?"

"Not even the district attorney?"

"Especially not Sebastion Primeaux." He took a

handkerchief from his pocket and wiped beads of sweat from his forehead. "Let's go sit in the car. It's too damn hot out here for this conversation."

Georgette doubted the car would make this conversation any more palatable.

TANNER KNEW the risk involved with what he was about to do. The Confidential agency was effective in large part because so few people knew it existed.

But Georgette had been pulled into the danger, not only by him but by her own psychic powers. The whole idea of trances and visions was as foreign to him as a lecture on understanding women given in Chinese—or in English for that matter. But Georgette had led him to the double murder scene and Lily's necklace.

Conrad Burke had stressed that things were building to a head fast and time was of the essence in their investigation into the Nilian rebels. Now Lily appeared connected to the rebels in ways he didn't even want to imagine. At this point, neither he nor New Orleans Confidential could afford to lose Georgette's input.

Georgette reached the car before him and settled into the passenger seat while he slid behind the wheel. He cranked the car engine and the air-conditioning, then pushed his seat back so that he could turn and face her. Even in the heat, even after walking over dead bodies and stamping through the edge of the swamp, she looked good. Really good.

And, in spite of all her powers as an attorney and a psychic, she looked surprisingly vulnerable. He hated that he'd still have to be less than totally honest with her.

He didn't know any way to say this other than just to spit it out, so he took a deep breath and plunged in. "I'm an undercover agent working for a secret government agency."

Her eyebrows raised. "Are you serious?"

"Serious as a 'gator in your swimming pool."

"What kind of secret agency?"

"We look into situations that may not meet the criteria for other law enforcement agencies to get involved."

"You work outside the law?"

"Not too far outside. Kind of skirt the limits."

"Is this part of the Homeland Security Act?"

"No, but national security is a part of what we do."

"Then whatever you're investigating must have something to do with the man with the scorpion tattoo."

"I'm sorry, Georgette, but I'm not at liberty to name the agency or the assignment."

"Are you working with the NOPD?"

"It's not common knowledge, but the chief of police knows we're in town."

"But not the D.A.'s office?"

"Not that we're aware of." And this is where it got really sticky. "How long have you worked for Sebastion Primeaux?" he asked.

"Two years. I was hired on the day after my thirty-first birthday."

"What's your take on him?"

"As a person or as a D.A.?"

"Both."

"He's very competent. Usually easy to work with.

A family man.'' She met his gaze. ''Is Sebastion being investigated?''

He wasn't sure he should go this far. But he trusted
Georgette, and she could well be just the in they
needed to find out exactly what Sebastion was doing
to aid the mob boss.

''We have evidence that Sebastion is being blackmailed by Jerome Senegal.''

Shock registered on her face. ''You're wrong.
Sebastion would never get involved with such a
man.''

''The evidence against him is strong.''

''What grounds does Senegal have for blackmail?''

''I'm not at liberty to reveal that information.''

Her mouth flew open and fire danced in her dark
eyes. ''I can get shot at and dragged out to a crime
scene, but I can't know what's going on with my
boss?''

''Don't get bent out of shape. I didn't make the
rules. I'm just trying to follow them.''

''I never took you for a rule follower, Tanner Harrison.''

''Well, good, because I break a hell of a lot more
than I follow. I have reasons not to break this one.''

''Does Lily's being missing have something to do
with your assignment? Was she abducted to get back
at you?''

''Anything's possible, but I've told you the truth
about Lily from the very beginning. All I know is that
she worked for Maurice Gaspard and then disappeared.''

''Nice that you told me the truth about something.
Do you even work for Crescent City Transports?''

''In a way. It's my cover. Look, I know this is a

lot to deal with, Georgette, but I didn't go looking for you, remember? You found me.''

"Thanks to the visions. What were you before you went to work for this agency?''

"I was with the CIA for years. I quit a couple of months back when I burned out. I was away on assignment when Lily came to New Orleans looking for me. When I returned, I took this job.''

"How does one go about applying for a job with a secret agency?''

"You don't. The boss recruits. For some reason he thought I had the qualifications he was looking for. Said I was tenacious as a bulldog and too hardheaded to back down from a good fight.''

"I can see how he thought that. So, what's next, Tanner? We have bodies out here and we can't just walk off and leave them.''

"I don't plan to. And I hate even to ask you this under the circumstances, but I don't see any way around it.''

"What now?''

"I know I promised I wouldn't say a word to anyone about your psychic powers, but I need to explain the situation to my boss. You can trust him, and I can promise you the information won't leave our agency.''

"You can promise, but that doesn't guarantee it won't happen.'' She sighed and shrugged her shoulders. "But do what you have to, Tanner. I'm in too deep to back out now.''

"Thanks.'' He reached across the seat and took her hand in his. "I don't understand your gift, Georgette. I won't even pretend to. But if I find Lily alive, you'll be the reason. I can't tell you what that means to me.''

They sat there for a few minutes, neither saying anything, though he felt closer to her right now than he'd felt to anyone in a long time, maybe ever. It scared him. Emotions always did.

And now he needed to get her out of here. "I'm going to make a couple of phone calls and catch my boss and my partner up on the morning's events," Tanner said. "Then I'll get someone to drive out here and help collect what evidence we can before I notify the local authorities that there's been a double murder."

"How long will that take?"

"Most of the day, I'm guessing, since we're so far out of town. But there's no reason for you to stay any longer," he said, finally letting go of her hand. "You can take my car back to New Orleans. I'll get my partner to drop me off at your place later to pick it up."

She crawled out of the car and met him on the driver's side. He held the door open for her, but instead of getting in, she stood there, so close he could feel her breath on his hot, sticky face.

"I know I hit you with a lot," he said.

"You did, but actually it makes sense of a lot of things that didn't add up."

"Then you believe me?"

"The secret agency bit is a tad over the top, but, yeah. Call me crazy, but I believe you."

"Good. We'll talk more later." He wiped a speck of dirt from her cheek, and the feel of her soft flesh did strange things to his senses.

"Lily's lucky to have you for a father," she said.

"She doesn't think that."

"Only because she doesn't really know you."

Georgette raised to her tiptoes and pressed her soft lips to his bruised ones. The kiss was only a friendly peck but his heart knocked around in his chest.

''Be careful, Tanner,'' she whispered. ''And thanks for leveling with me. It makes all of this easier to deal with—I think.'' She didn't wait for him to answer, just got in the car and buckled the seat belt.

She was one hell of a woman. Way too good for him. She'd realize that soon enough.

GEORGETTE PULLED OFF I-10 at a truck stop a few miles east of Beau Bridge, in dire need of a caffeine fix. It was one thirty in the afternoon and she hadn't eaten since the chicken salad last night. She was feeling a few hunger pains but wasn't certain her stomach was ready for food after the dive it had taken at the murder scene.

She parked and went inside, heading straight to the bathroom to wash her hands. Fortunately, the restroom was clean and there was lots of soap. She hit the dispenser knob several times, then scrubbed until she was certain nothing of the dirt and stench of Crazy Eugene's could possibly remain on them.

That done, she found a booth near the back of the café and ordered black coffee and a bowl of soup. She leaned back and tried to unwind, but thoughts were flying at her much too fast and in random order. What a morning. What a week.

Ever since she'd run into Tanner the other night at the hospital, her life had been one wild roller-coaster ride. She couldn't trust her emotions when her adrenaline level was at a constant high. Nor could she ignore them.

The attraction she felt for Tanner was growing so

strong it frightened her, especially since she had no way of validating anything he told her. A secret agent for a shadowy organization. A man who posed as a truck driver but was dealing with the most dangerous criminal element in New Orleans. A man who...

...who made her heart race with a touch.

The waitress returned with the coffee and Georgette wondered if the sudden flash of heat she felt inside her showed on her face.

"Soup will be right up. Sure you don't want a sandwich to go with it?"

"No, thanks."

Georgette sipped the coffee, trying to think about Tanner and his recent revelations with more objectivity. His story was bizarre, yet she believed he was telling the truth. And not just because she was attracted to him. This was more of a metaphysical feeling, side effects of the gift that had a way of insinuating itself into her life whether she welcomed it or not.

And if Tanner was telling the truth about his identity, it was also very likely that he had the inside track on Sebastion Primeaux. It was difficult to believe the accusation of blackmail was accurate, but it would explain a lot of things—like Sebastion's volatile disposition of late and the lost evidence on Tony Arsenault.

She pulled out her notebook and started scribbling notes, barely glancing up when the waitress put the soup on her table and refilled her coffee cup.

She flipped to the next page in her notebook and started drawing. Without thinking about it, she was sketching facial features of Sebastion, stern and serious, the way he looked when he faced a jury for his final arguments.

She didn't do justice to his eyes, but she got the nose right. Classic. The mouth was easy. Thin lips. Strong jaw lines. Basically, Sebastion was a good-looking guy, sophisticated and nice-looking for a man in his fifties.

He had everything going for him, and he liked it that way. So where had he slipped up? What did Senegal have on him?

The waitress reappeared with a refill. "You must be an artist."

"No. I just sketch when I'm thinking the way some people doodle."

"You're good at it." She stepped closer and peered at the sketch. "That looks just like a guy who was in here earlier. Exactly like him, in fact. He sat right over there, second booth. Nervous. Didn't eat anything, but drank half a pot of black coffee and kept glancing out the window."

"Take a closer look," Georgette said, handing the notebook to the waitress. "Do you still think you saw this man in here earlier today?"

"If it wasn't him, it was his twin."

"Was he alone?"

"Sure was. I thought he was waiting on someone the way he kept looking out the window, but if he was, the person didn't show."

"What time was that?"

"I don't know exactly. Early. I'd guess around eight o'clock."

Georgette waved off the refill. She retrieved her wallet and placed a ten-dollar bill next to her coffee cup. "This should cover everything."

"Easy." The waitress picked up the money. "I'll get your change."

"That's okay. You keep it." She slid from the booth and headed for the door. She was certain Sebastion had nothing to do with the murders. They were too brutal. He would never have the stomach for that. But then, before today she wouldn't have thought him capable of any kind of dealings with Jerome Senegal.

And to think she'd complained just last weekend that her life was dull.

Tony Arsenault parked his car at the back of the old warehouse on Tchoupitoulas. He'd promised Senegal he'd get started refining the drugs today and Tony was a man of his word. Just don't push him. When guys pushed him, he got really pissed and then he never knew what he'd do.

He'd been pushed way too hard this morning. There was no call for that Nilian scorpion bum to kill Eugene. No cause at all. Yet he'd put a bullet through Eugene's head and had been about to force himself on Lily when Tony had walked in and found them.

Tony clenched his hands into fists, remembering the feel of the knife in his hands when he'd taken care of Raoul. But even that hadn't satisfied him. He was sick of the rebels, not just Raoul but all of them. Hanging around. Giving orders. They'd be furious now, but they'd never know it was Tony who'd killed Raoul. The only person who knew that was Lily, and she wouldn't be talking.

He walked around the car and unlocked the trunk, scanning the area quickly to make sure no one was around to see what he was about to take out of there and dump in the river behind the warehouse. It wouldn't do to let Jerome find out that Tony had gone against his orders and taken care of Lily himself. Jerome Senegal did not tolerate being crossed.

Chapter Ten

Georgette knew something was wrong the second she pushed through the door of her condo. It was a feeling and the odor of aftershave. She started to close the door and go for security. That's when she noticed Sebastion Primeaux.

Sebastion casually folded the copy of the *Times Picayune* he'd been reading, set the newspaper on the corner of the coffee table and stood to greet her.

"How did you get into my condo?" Georgette demanded, furious, yet not so much so that she wasn't aware of the prickles of apprehension that crawled up and down her spine.

"I have a key and the code. You gave them to me last fall when you were in Austin for your friend's wedding."

She remembered now. There had been a hurricane in the Gulf and she'd wanted him to check on her condo in case they got damaging winds. But last fall she hadn't suspected him of being connected with the mob.

"I didn't think you'd mind if I waited for you inside," he said. "If I was wrong, I'm sorry."

She took a deep breath and tried to think how best

to handle this. "I don't mind. It's just that it's a bit unnerving to walk in and find someone here." She'd make sure she got the key back before he left and later have maintenance change the locks on her door. "Is this about one of our cases?"

He nodded. "We need to talk about the evidence against Tony Arsenault."

He shuffled his feet and looked everywhere but straight at her, very uncharacteristic behavior for Sebastion.

"Would you mind if I fixed myself a drink?" he asked, finally meeting her gaze. "I could use one."

"No problem. Vodka, gin or Scotch. That's pretty much the extent of my choices." She seldom drank hard liquor, but kept a limited supply on hand for friends who did.

He followed her to the kitchen, his hands in his pockets rattling his keys. Questions played in her mind as she took a highball glass down from the shelf and opened the door to the pantry where the liquor was stored.

"Did you have a busy day?" she asked as she dropped a couple of cubes of ice into his glass.

"I spent last night in Lafayette and drove back early this morning."

Which would have placed him on I-10 and explained his coffee break in the truck stop. "I hope the trip was for pleasure and not more work," she said, digging for more information.

"It was a little of both. I was helping a good friend plan the defense of a very high-profile client. He wanted input from a prosecutor's standpoint, so he'd be better prepared."

She fixed herself a glass of ice water. "We can talk in here," she said.

He twirled his drink, still avoiding eye contact. "You've done a great job over the last two years, Georgette. You have more promise than any junior prosecutor on the staff."

"I'm sure you didn't come over on Saturday to tell me that. So what's the bad news?"

He frowned. "Guess I'm too obvious. It's the media thing. They're up in arms about Arsenault's release from jail. So is the mayor."

"They should be."

"I know, and I wish I had explanations for them. The mayor's called a press conference for ten o'clock Monday morning. He wants me to make a statement."

"What can you say other than the fact that the evidence has disappeared?"

"That's the problem. The mayor won't accept that. He wants me to explain how the evidence is protected when it's in our office. That means I have to admit that you were the last person to handle the evidence against Tony."

"I was the last person to sign out the evidence file. That doesn't mean I was the last to handle it."

"I know. I'm not blaming you, but I'm sure the media will take the story and run with it." He spread his palms as a symbol of exasperation. "I hate to do this, but I don't see any way out. I'm going to have to put you on paid suspension until this is settled. It's the only thing the media, the mayor and the public will accept."

"So this is how it's going to be? You know I'm innocent, but you're making me the fall guy."

"It's just temporary, Georgette."

Temporary or not this would be a black mark on her career. No matter what came out later, people would only remember that she'd been responsible for lost evidence against a nefarious mobster. Evidence that Sebastion had most likely destroyed to appease Jerome Senegal. She fought the urge to dump her glass of ice water on his head.

"I'd like my key back now, Sebastion, and I'd like you to leave."

"This isn't personal, Georgette. I hope you realize that."

"Wrong. It's as personal as it gets."

"I hoped you would understand, but I see that was too much to ask."

"Get out."

"One other thing. I have to insist that you stay away from the office until you're reinstated."

"I have personal things there that I need."

"You can pick them up Monday morning, but someone will accompany you to the office and see you out of the building when you've finished. Again, it's not personal. That's the official policy when someone is fired or put on suspension."

"By all means, let's be official." She put out her hand. "My key."

He pulled his key ring from his pocket, removed her silver key and laid it on the table. "I am sorry about all this, Georgette. Really sorry. I had no choice. I hope you know that."

Strangely enough, he did sound sorry. The rest was a lie. He had a choice. There was no proof at all that she'd done anything wrong, and her record was spotless.

She didn't walk him to the door. He'd found his way in. He could find his way out. She'd trusted Sebastion and he'd used her to cover his own sins. But then why should that shock her now? He'd given up all claims to decency or ethics when he'd let himself become embroiled with criminals.

She went to the door, turned the deadbolt, then collapsed onto the sofa. For all her psychic powers, she hadn't seen this coming, nor had she had a clue before today that Sebastion had switched sides in the war against crime.

Naive. That was the only word to describe her. Those days were over.

But then so were the days when she had a job.

Her whole life had changed since her life had become intricately entangled with Tanner Harrison. You'd think she'd be angry at him, but the truth was, she already missed him and couldn't wait for him to walk through her door.

Still, she didn't need a psychic revelation to know there was no chance for them to establish a real relationship. He needed her powers now, but sane men didn't want permanent relationships with women who fell into trances and saw visions.

That was one more thing she'd learned at her mother's knee.

TONY WALKED THROUGH the warehouse with Senegal, looking over the raw material and examining the refining equipment. "It seems to be all here," he said, anxious for Senegal to be on his way.

As usual, the boss's timing had been perfect. Tony had just unlocked and opened the trunk to his car when Senegal had driven up. He'd panicked for a minute, sure Senegal had gotten the word about the murders and was going to come down on him.

But apparently Senegal hadn't gotten the word yet. He was nervous, though, and Tony hadn't seen the boss nervous too often.

"I need this stuff up and running fast," Senegal said. "Don't let me down. I'm counting on you."

"Sure, boss, you can always count on me."

"You're the man, Tony. You're the man." Senegal clapped him on the back.

It was just the two of them in the warehouse, though Senegal's usual throng of bodyguards were outside waiting on him. That was what worried Tony. He'd drugged Lily to keep her quiet on the way back from Eugene's, but she'd be coming to any minute. If she started moaning or knocking around in the car, one of them might hear her.

He should have killed her then and there, but had decided it was better to throw her into the river. Let her just wash up the way the other prostitutes had. That way there would be no way Tanner Harrison could tie her in with Butcher and Raoul or have any evidence that tied Tony to her death.

"What's the status on the deal with Ricardo Gonzalez and his scorpion thugs?" Tony asked, as he steered Senegal toward the exit.

"A cargo ship from Nilia with a new supply of drugs will be docking in a couple of days. Gonzalez and his motley rebel crew plan to leave on it whether I deliver or not. If I don't deliver, they'll take the drugs and look for someone who can."

"How close are you to meeting their demands?"

"I'm still a couple of million dollars off the mark.

I could make half of that back tonight if I had the refined drugs in my hand.''

"You can't pick up that kind of money on the streets.''

"No. We're moving up in the world. Playing with the big-time boys out of Chicago. They heard about what we've got and they want in on the action. A drug that heightens sexual desire and is more addictive than crack or heroin—they want it. And we're the only game in the country, unless we lose our source.''

"Gotcha, boss man. Guess I better get to work.''

He'd already started dumping a batch of the raw product when he heard the commotion at the door. He spun around just in time to see Lily Harrison spit into the face of one of Senegal's biggest bodyguards. The hellcat was awake.

LILY'S HEAD felt as if it were splitting into fragments and bouncing around inside her skull. She had no idea what day it was anymore or what would come at her next.

She tried to pull away from the giant baboon who had a death grip on her arm, but even if she hadn't been woozy from whatever the guy called Tony had shot into her arm, she'd still be no match for this guy.

Jerome Senegal spat out a stream of curse words that would have shocked Lily a couple of months ago. Nothing shocked her anymore.

"Where did you find her?'' Senegal demanded.

"Packed away in the trunk of Arsenault's car.''

Senegal grabbed the collar of Arsenault's shirt. "I told you to leave Lily to me.''

"She's my problem, Senegal. I'm the one she can finger for murder."

And now she could finger him for murdering Raoul. There was no way she would get out of this alive.

"Where's Butcher?"

"I don't know. The last time I saw him he was heading out into the swamps to find Lily. He let her get away. I found her and brought her back with me."

Senegal let go of Tony's shirt collar. "Are you sure that's all there is to this?"

"It's all I know." He shot Lily a warning look, and she decided talking now was not to her advantage. She knew all too well what Tony Arsenault was capable of.

"I'll take her from here," Senegal said.

"Why? I've got empty rooms here. I'll lock her in one of them."

"I want her alive," Senegal said. "If this blows up in our face, she may be our only ticket out. Tanner Harrison will do whatever it takes to keep her alive, even if that means buying time for us to leave the country."

Lily bit her tongue but still she couldn't keep quiet. "My daddy won't help you bastards."

"Sure he will, sweetheart. He'll sit up and beg like a pitiful little poodle to save you."

"Are you buying time for *us* to leave, Senegal? Or for you to leave?" Tony asked.

"I take care of my own."

"I'd feel a whole lot better about your remembering that if I have Lily in my hands. If she talks, it's my ass that faces a death sentence and that two-bit

D.A. you're jerking the strings on won't be able to stop it.''

"You still don't get it, do you, Tony? If she talks, the party's over. We'll all go to prison. I'm not crazy enough to let that happen. She's dead either way. For that matter, so is Tanner. But we'll do it on my time-table.''

"Fine. Your timetable, but she stays with me if you want these drugs ready to sell by morning. Let Tanner Harrison keep poking his nose around the Quarter. There's no way he'll find her here.''

Her father was looking for her.

Lily grabbed and held on to that fact. If he was looking for her, he must love her. He must. No matter what her mother had told her. She'd hang on as long as she could just for the chance of seeing him again.

Tears wet her eyes, and she didn't fight back as she was pushed into a dirty bathroom. The door was slammed shut behind her and she heard a key click in the lock.

But she'd escaped in the swamp and she'd do it again. This time she'd be successful. And even if she wasn't, her father would find her and he'd make these men pay. He'd make them all pay.

She bit back her tears. She couldn't waste her energy feeling sorry for herself. She needed it to survive.

IT WAS NEARLY seven in the evening by the time Tanner made it back to Georgette's condo complex. He'd had Mason stop by his apartment long enough for him to shower and change into clean clothes that didn't have the stench of death on them.

Mason said all the right things, but Tanner still

didn't trust him. Men didn't change. Once a criminal, always a criminal. He'd found that out in his years with the CIA. Sometimes they went clean for years, but when trouble broke out, the best place to start looking for the cause was in old police records.

Conrad Burke didn't see it that way. He was a lot more optimistic about a lot of things than Tanner was. But then Burke had it all—the perfect wife, the perfect family.

Tanner had always been a loser where women were concerned. He'd tried to turn it around with his marriage to Juliana, but in the end she had ripped Lily from his life and put an ocean between them. Even then he'd been left with hope. If he lost his daughter this time, there would be none.

GEORGETTE SAT on the sofa. Tanner paced, clearly as aggravated and concerned as she was by Sebastion's visit and the latest development in a deadly situation that was almost as baffling to her as it was frightening.

"Do you think it's possible Sebastion committed those murders?" she asked.

"Anything's possible, but it's not likely. The bullet through the head at close range was hitman style. The repeated stabbing that bordered on mutilation is usually a passion killing or committed by someone with a taste for blood and gore."

"Then you think Sebastion was telling the truth about why he was in the area?"

"I wouldn't go that far. Lying's become a way of life to the guy."

"So it seems." She readjusted the throw pillow and scooted back, pulling her feet up beside her on the couch. "Sebastion is working at cross purposes with everything he's claimed to be trying to accomplish. And I was too big a fool to see it."

"The guy's taken in an entire electorate, so there's no reason for you to beat up on yourself."

"No. I'll wait and let the media do that for me. When the powerful D.A. tells them I've been relieved of my duties, they'll run with the story and everyone will assume I'm guilty. Once again, he'll come out looking like the dedicated district attorney."

Tanner stopped pacing and perched on the arm of the sofa. "He could have another purpose for putting you on suspension."

"Like what?"

"It would get you out of the office so that you can't snoop around and find out what's really going on."

She gave the comment some thought. "He did say I couldn't be there alone anymore."

"Did he take your key?"

"Not yet, but I only have a key to my office, not to the building. Sebastion's probably alerted security not to let me in the building except during regular hours."

"Is there always a security guard on duty?" Tanner asked.

"Always."

"That makes breaking in difficult, but not impossible."

"No. Don't even think about it, Tanner. If I get caught breaking and entering, Sebastion will see that I'm disbarred."

"I'll do the actual break-in. All I need from you is information."

"What kind of information?"

"Location of evidence files, location of Sebastion's personal files, computer passwords and file names—that kind of stuff," Tanner said. "And I'll need to know how to bypass the alarm system. You do know how to bypass the alarm system, don't you?"

"No," she answered, "well except for the back door. We still have a couple of smokers in the building and we have a thirty-second code so they can sneak in and out the back door for a quick cigarette. But they have to buzz to be let back in."

"That could work," he said. "I know you're in a small three-story building in the warehouse district. Do you share the building with other government agencies?"

"No. We have all three floors. The mail room and offices for the clerical staff are on the first floor. Sebastion and senior level attorneys have offices on the third floor. The rest of us are on the second floor."

Tanner nodded. "That's workable."

With all she'd been through in the last twenty-four hours, a break-in should be a piece of cake, but the whole idea made her extremely nervous. She didn't run yellow lights or drive over the speed limit. Didn't even cheat on her taxes—well barely cheated. Breaking and entering was downright criminal.

"Exactly what are you looking for?" she asked, hoping for a reason to justify this with her own conscience.

"Information about what Senegal's up to right now and Sebastion's involvement in those plans. And a lead to finding Lily."

Everything always went back to his daughter. "You really love Lily, don't you?"

"I'm her father."

"Being a father doesn't guarantee love."

"Then, yes, I love her. How does Sunday afternoon sound for a break-in?"

"So soon?"

"I thought about tonight, but after all that's happened the last twenty-four hours, I'm not sure my mental state is at its sharpest."

"Why afternoon? Why not wait until dark?"

"The security guard may be less stringent in his patrols during daylight hours. And I won't have to worry about his noticing the beam of a flashlight or hearing me stumble around in the dark. Besides, I have the beginnings of a plan in my mind, and it would work a lot better during daylight hours."

But it would still be risky—and dangerous. They could be arrested and carted off to jail. Her career could be ruined, if it wasn't already. Worse, the security guard was armed. She couldn't imagine him shooting her after all the times they'd made small talk when she'd worked late nights and weekends, but who knew what Sebastion had told him?

"No" was on the tip of her tongue, until she thought of Lily and the silver necklace with the dangling silver heart. Lily was only seventeen, had run away from home and traveled to America to see her father, only to face prostitution and abduction.

And there were so many others. Young runaways lured into Senegal's world of intimidation and degradation, of drugs and blatant immorality, like the young woman who'd been beaten and left to die in a lonely courtyard in the Quarter.

"I'm up for it. In fact, I'm going in with you, Tanner."

"No." He left the arm of the sofa and took a seat next to her. "You said yourself the action can get you disbarred."

"I'll take that risk."

Tanner placed a thumb beneath her chin and tilted her face to meet his penetrating gaze. "Listen to me, Georgette. I appreciate your offer, but I can't let you do this."

"You're not *letting* me. It's my choice, but don't worry. I'm not doing it for you. I'm doing it for Lily and all the other underage prostitutes whose lives Jerome Senegal has taken or ruined. And I'm doing it for me, so I can live with myself after being part of Sebastion Primeaux's team."

Tanner dropped her hand and started pacing again, so full of restless energy she thought he might erupt like a smouldering volcano.

"I'm on for tomorrow, Tanner, but you have to go home now. If I experience any psychic phenomena that concerns Lily, I'll call you, but we both need some down time."

He stopped pacing and stared at her. "I can live with the second half of that."

"If you want my help in any of this, you'll agree to my being on the scene when you break into Sebastion's office."

He glared at her. "Are all female attorneys this bossy or is this a psychic thing?"

"It's a Georgette Delacroix thing." He would never willingly agree to her going with him, but she'd made up her mind. If there was evidence in the D.A.'s office that could bring down the mob's New Orleans empire, she'd find it.

With or without her psychic powers. With or without Tanner. But she knew Sunday would come much too soon.

"DELIVERY FOR Sebastion Primeaux."

The security guard looked Tanner over and must have decided he looked legitimate in his uniform with Crescent City Transports engraved over the left front pocket. "I'll take it."

"This is just part of it. I'll have to use the dolly to bring in the rest. Looks like somebody's getting a fancy new office chair." Tanner handed him a clipboard with a fake order sheet. "Just sign anywhere that you're taking delivery."

The guard scrawled his name across the bottom of the page. "Kind of unusual to make deliveries on Sunday afternoon, isn't it?"

"Yeah, and don't I love it? Double-time pay. I wish we were this busy every week."

"You hiring drivers over there?"

"Not that I know of, but guys come and go all the time. You looking for a job?"

"Yeah, for my brother-in-law so he can stop freeloading off of me."

They both laughed, and Tanner headed back to the truck to get the huge box of packing material loaded on the dolly. So far it was going exactly as planned. The mail room where weekend and after-hour deliveries were kept was just a few steps from the back door.

Tanner would need only a few minutes by himself to turn off the alarm, release the door locks and let Georgette sneak in with his supplies. Then as soon as he was out the front door, he'd move the truck out of sight, sneak around to the back and join her.

If the guard didn't give him the opportunity he needed to unlock the back door, this would get a lot more complicated. Tanner didn't want gunplay, but if necessary, he'd try to take the guard by surprise and inject the tranquilizer he'd brought from the Confidential office.

That would keep him quiet long enough for them to go through Sebastion's office and check his private files, but it would make it a lot more likely that Sebastion would discover the surprises Tanner planned to leave behind.

The guard was on the phone when Tanner returned with the rest of the pseudo order and only interrupted his conversation long enough to point out the mail room and send Tanner off in the right direction.

There were still any number of things that could go wrong, especially with that pistol resting on the guard's hip. Tanner would feel better about this if Georgette weren't with him, but he knew his chances of success were ninety percent better with her along.

Still, knowing he'd be putting her in harm's way made him nervous. And every undercover agent knew that nervousness could lead to deadly mistakes.

Chapter Eleven

Each creak of the wood or thud of her tennis shoes sounded like thunder to Georgette as she and Tanner crept up the back staircase. "I don't know how professional burglars take the stress," she whispered as they finally closed the door of the stairwell behind them.

"You're doing great," Tanner whispered back.

"Where do you want to start?"

"In Sebastion's office."

"It's probably locked."

"Secret agents and burglars don't worry about such mundane problems."

She led the way around the corner, past the elevator and to the closed door. Tanner produced a gadget from the small leather satchel he'd had her sneak inside for him and fitted the pointed end into the keyhole. A few turns, a few clicks and the instrument locked into place. A turn of the knob, and the door opened.

"That's all it takes to get inside a locked room!"

"That's all it takes if you have the right tools. This is state of the art."

He closed the door and locked it again. "If the

guard makes rounds, he'll likely only check the door. If he does, don't make a sound.''

''But what if he unlocks it and comes in to look around?''

''Then duck behind the desk and leave the confrontation to me.''

She swallowed hard. ''He has a gun.''

''So do I. I don't plan for either of us to use them. Chances are good that he won't open the door unless he hears something and we'll hear his footsteps before he gets close enough to hear our whispers. He weighs over two hundred pounds and he walks with a heavy foot.''

She sincerely hoped Tanner was right. More worried than ever, she went straight to Sebastion's desk and turned on his computer. Tanner got busy with the desk drawers, unlocking each one.

''Can we lock them back when we're through?''

''Yes, and he'll never know they were touched. That's the beauty of this instrument. Start with the drawers, then we'll move to the computer files.''

''What do I look for?''

''Nilia, Scorpion Poison, Ricardo Gonzalez, Jerome Senegal, or anything that looks suspicious to you.''

So she'd been right. The scorpion was more than a random tattoo. She'd demand more information later, but now she just wanted to get done and get out. Her hand trembled as she opened the wide center drawer, afraid of what she'd find, more afraid that she'd find nothing.

There were only the usual office supplies, pretty similar to what was in her own top drawer except that Sebastion had a bottle of antacids in his—and a nose hair trimmer. When she looked up, Tanner was standing on a chair attaching something that looked like a small screw head to the inside of one of the track lighting deflectors.

"It's a camera," Tanner explained, when he saw her staring.

"That small?"

"But powerful. It will show the food stuck between Sebastion's teeth."

"He flosses after a donut." Still the technology amazed her. "How will you view the pictures? Don't tell me it transmits back to your office."

"No, but it will transmit up to three hundred yards. The truck we're in is actually a highly specialized surveillance vehicle. That's why I had you bring the car. I'll park the truck within that perimeter and we'll be in business, as long as Sebastion doesn't discover the camera and have it removed."

"How would he ever find it? It looks as if it's part of the lighting."

"Senegal has equipment that would detect it. Sebastion may as well, since he seems to be a major player in the game. That's why we want to leave everything exactly as we found it. Give him no reason to debug."

She progressed to the side drawers. The top one was more of the same—colored markers, a supply of sticky notes, extra staples, a sleeve of golf balls someone had brought him from Pebble Beach...and a box of condoms. How many married men kept condoms in their desk drawer, she wondered as she closed that drawer and opened the bottom one.

As in most office desks, the drawer was designed to hold files. She used hers for her handbag and a small makeup kit, but Sebastion's contained neatly labeled manila folders. She quickly skimmed the tabs, stopping at one labeled Tony Arsenault.

She pulled the file and examined the contents. It was all there—copies of everything that Sebastion had claimed was lost plus even more information on Tony's other dirty dealings.

"Take a look at this," she whispered.

Tanner joined her at the desk, and she handed him the file, saying "Just as we suspected. He deliberately let Arsenault go free."

Tanner skimmed the material.

"Should I make copies?" she asked, wanting proof that she wasn't the one responsible for letting The Knife back on the streets.

"Too risky. The guard might hear the machine." He reached into his satchel and took out a camera only a little larger than a postage stamp and started snapping pictures of each page.

"Keep looking," he said, "but work quickly." He handed her the camera when he'd finished. "Use this to make photos of anything you think is of value."

She went back to scanning the drawer. Tanner walked over to the file cabinet and took the back off a silver-framed picture of Sebastion's wife and two children.

"Not another camera," she said.

"Yes, but this one has audio, too, so we'll be able to see anything we miss on the other camera and hear even the lowest whisper. All I have to do is make an indiscernible pinhole in his wife's eye for the camera to view through."

"A pinhole? That means anyone could be watched twenty-four hours a day and never know it."

She shuddered at the thought and knew she'd never feel as if she had complete privacy again. Still, she went back to the files, this time pulling out a folder marked Confidential. It was thicker than the others and when she opened it, a couple of photographs spilled out, slid off the desk and landed in her lap.

She picked one up, then dropped it to the desk in revulsion. Sebastion was front and center, shirtless and his pants were unzipped and hanging open. He was standing in the midst of a group of nude and semi-nude young women, none of whom appeared to be much over the age of sixteen, and at least one who looked to be as young as twelve. They had their hands all over him. He cradled the breast of one girl and the derriere of another.

Georgette clamped her hand over her mouth as her stomach rolled and pitched. So this was what he'd done to leave himself wide-open to blackmail.

"What's wrong?" Tanner asked, obviously noticing that she was turning green.

"Pictures of Sebastion in the midst of an orgy."

"I was hoping you didn't have to see those."

"I wish I hadn't." Her thoughts flew to Sebastion's wife and two adorable children, one a daughter not much younger than the females he was pictured with. "It will break his wife's heart if she ever sees these."

"I'm sure Sebastion knows that. They'll also end his career."

"Senegal has him by the balls."

"And no one walks away from Jerome Senegal."

"I know," Georgette said. "I've seen the bodies of young prostitutes who've tried."

She went back to the task at hand with a vengeance, but none of the other files set off any kind of alarms. Closing the drawer quietly, she clicked the computer mouse and went to the file menu while Tanner installed yet another bug, this one into the phone.

She typed in the word *Nilia,* then hit Browse. No matching files were found. The same happened with *Gonzalez* and *Scorpion Poison.* There were files on Jerome Senegal, but they were the same ones available to all the prosecutors in the office.

She went back to the main menu and began searching for additional files. When prompted for a password, she typed frantically, using dates and names Sebastion might have chosen because of their association to his life. Anniversary date, children's birthdays, his birthday and combinations thereof. Nothing worked.

"Shut it down," Tanner said. "Let's get out of here with what we have."

"We don't have much."

"But we have equipment in place."

"Okay, James Bond." She shut down the computer while Tanner returned his tools to the satchel.

"Just about there," he whispered as they left the office and started down the hallway.

They'd just turned the corner when they heard the elevator bell, followed by voices—Sebastion's and one she didn't recognize. They froze to the spot until they heard the clatter of keys and the opening and closing of an office door, most likely Sebastion's.

Georgette's pulse skyrocketed. They'd come within seconds of being caught in the act.

"Go back to the car," Tanner said. "Drive away but stay in the area. I'll call you when I have the truck parked in an out-of-the-way spot."

"Why are you telling me that now?"

"Because that's Jerome Senegal with Sebastion. I'm going back to the door and see if I can hear part of the conversation going on in that room."

"I thought you could eavesdrop from the truck?"

"I can, once the equipment is up and running. That will take a while."

"It's too dangerous, Tanner."

"It's my job, Georgette. If I worried about danger, I'd be a car salesman." He squeezed her hand. "I'll be fine. Now go, before the guard makes his rounds and discovers both of us."

She did as he ordered, but her fear for him escalated to the point that she could barely breathe as she crept down the stairs and turned off the alarm at the back door. There was no sign of the guard as she let herself out. Tanner had told her to drive away, but she couldn't. Not until she knew he was out of the building safely, so she pulled her car to a spot where she could watch the exit but wouldn't be noticed.

This was Tanner's job. He chose to do this kind of thing for a living. There was no excuse for her to be so panicky.

No excuse, but there was a reason. A very stupid, irresponsible reason. She was falling for the man, falling hard.

TANNER POSITIONED HIMSELF just outside the door, facing the elevator so he'd know if someone else joined the meeting in progress in Sebastion's office. Reaching into the leather satchel, he removed a small audio magnifying device that when attached to the door would help him hear the conversation clearly. Not a tool he'd expected to need today.

"I don't like meeting on Sunday, Jerome, especially not here in my office."

"You take care of business, or you won't have an office to worry about."

"I can't make them give up the goods when we don't have the cash."

"We'll have the cash by 8:00 a.m. Close the deal, Sebastion, and then I have one more little job for you to take care of. The instructions are all here."

Tanner heard the rattling of paper, then a few seconds of silence.

"No. I've gone along with everything else you've asked, but I can't do this."

"I'm not asking, Sebastion. I'm telling you."

"It's going too far."

"What part of this operation do you think isn't going too far? You're handling negotiations for a deal that will guarantee the slaughter of thousands of innocent people. And now you get cold feet over the death of one?"

"But this is different."

"You should have thought about that a hundred prostitutes ago."

"I want out, Jerome. I've had enough. Do what you want to with the pictures and the videos. And with me. Just go ahead and kill me right now if that's what you want to do."

"Oh, no. That would be far too easy—for you. You back out of this now, and I'll deliver your wife and kids to you, one by one. Gift-wrapped. In pieces you can put together like a friggin' puzzle. Sleep with that thought tonight, Sebastion, and give me your answer in the morning."

Senegal's footsteps moved toward the door. Tanner

managed to get around the corner a tenth of a second before the office door opened and Senegal stepped into the hall. Sebastion was clearly involved in more than intentionally losing evidence. He was playing a major part in Senegal's relations with the Nilian rebels. That had to be what the slaughter of thousands referred to.

The odds were probably a million to one that he'd also do whatever it was Senegal wanted from him now. Unless Tanner and the Confidential agents stopped him first.

The bugs he'd just implanted in Sebastion's office might give them the edge they were looking for. Who'd have thought Georgette Delacroix might turn out to be the break they'd needed all along?

But he'd also pulled her into danger. He'd do anything in his power to keep her safe, but he'd felt the same about Lily, and he was failing her the way he'd failed everyone in his life who'd ever mattered.

The old hurts came back and mingled with the new fears. And underneath it all was the growing knowledge that what he felt for Georgette went deeper than he could handle right now. He jumped in his truck and grabbed the phone to let her know he'd made it out safely.

The phone rang before he could punch in the number. He glanced at the ID. Juliana. Good timing because she had some explaining to do. He listened to her tirade as he started the surveillance truck and pulled away from the hidden parking spot behind the district attorney's office. Her accusations cut him to the quick as always, but didn't curb his own anger.

"Why did you lie about the necklace I sent for Lily's birthday?"

"I don't know what you're talking about."

"You said she tossed it in the trash. You told me she said she wanted nothing from me."

"She did, but it's your own fault. You were never a father to her. Never."

"She didn't trash the necklace."

"How do you know? Have you seen her? Have you seen Lily?"

"No, but I found the necklace."

"This is a ridiculous argument, Tanner. I don't give a royal fig about that bloody necklace. I only want to know Lily's safe. If you were a decent father, it's all you'd want to know, too."

It was the same argument they'd had for years. He was a failure as a father. Juliana was the perfect mother. How could he doubt it? But this time he couldn't let go.

"You lied about the necklace, Juliana. What else did you lie about?"

"I won't have this ridiculous conversation with you while my daughter is missing."

"*Our* daughter."

"I didn't lie to you, Tanner. It's just that Lily has a wild streak in her. That's why she took off and came to America. It's not about you."

He didn't know if she was telling the truth or not, but he couldn't argue with her anymore. It wouldn't change anything anyway.

"I have to go. I'll call you the second I have news."

She sobbed into the phone. Tanner envied her the relief of crying. He didn't have that luxury. Men seldom did.

He'd have to make a call to Burke and fill him in

on the details of the afternoon's work. Before he could punch in the number, his phone rang again. This time it was Georgette.

"Did you find out anything?" she asked.

"The visitor was Jerome Senegal. I didn't get any specifics, but I heard part of their conversation. Why don't you go back to your place? I'll come by later and fill you in on the details."

"Where are you going?"

"To set up the surveillance receptors."

"You're not dumping me now that the fun is starting. Besides you were the one who wanted to stay stuck to me all weekend."

"Was that this weekend? It seems eons ago."

And the weekend wasn't over yet.

HAD GEORGETTE just been walking by, she would never have noticed the slightly dirty white delivery truck, much less have suspected it was a high-tech surveillance vehicle. At least not until she moved from the cab to the interior.

"Wow! This is some setup."

"The fun part of the job," Tanner admitted, beaming. "The part we're in now has its own cooling and lighting system and bathroom facilities, so it's totally self-contained. It's great for stakeouts."

It also had two leather swivel chairs that faced a wall of elaborate machinery and what appeared to be TV sets. Georgette watched in awe as Tanner fooled with wires and connections, turned knobs and adjusted a series of eight monitors mounted on the walls of the van.

"I had no idea trucks like this existed," she said,

as the first monitor flashed a series of horizontal lines across the screen.

"These were specially made."

"For the secret investigation that you're involved with?"

"For the agency and whatever investigations it becomes involved in."

Tanner fiddled with the controls until the lines were replaced by a shot of Sebastion's office. She stared, impressed by the detail that was visible even though the sun was low in the sky and the amount of light in the room was limited.

"Evidently Sebastion has left the building," she said.

"I'd still like to get all the monitors set up so the equipment is fully functioning in the morning."

"Will you just sit here all day tomorrow and monitor Sebastion?"

"Someone will. We'll likely take shifts."

"Can you pull up the pictures taken by the cameras while Sebastion was still in the room?"

"No. This control activates the cameras." He pointed to one of the machines he'd been working with. "This is primarily a video setup. There's no film or hard copy unless I make a copy on this feedback player." He touched a knob and a red light started flashing on what looked like a mutant CD player.

"This doesn't sound fully legal."

"You planning to take us to court, counselor?"

"Guess not, since I was there when you bugged the office."

But this was a very sophisticated operation, equipped with the latest and no doubt extremely expensive technological spy toys. Whatever they were investigating had to have far-reaching ramifications.

She tried to remember what she knew about the country of Nilia that Tanner had mentioned during the break-in. It was a small South American country, a major oil exporter with lots of internal strife. Drug problems, too. She remembered reading about that not too long ago. Though she was pretty certain she'd never heard the term Scorpion Poison.

"Is the Scorpion Poison you talked about some kind of illegal drug or is that more of the secret information I can't be told?"

Tanner made a few more adjustments, brought up a clear picture on the second monitor, then turned to face her. "I just got off the phone with my supervisor. I told him about you."

"That I'm psychic?"

"I told him that yesterday. Today I told him how you'd helped bug Sebastion's office. He gave me the okay to share a little more information with you."

Which in her mind could only mean one thing. "What does he want from me?"

"Any help you can give."

"With finding Lily?"

"Or with Sebastion, Jerome Senegal, Ricardo Gonzalez or Scorpion Poison. They're all related, and in spite of all our sophisticated equipment and manpower, we aren't getting the job done fast enough."

"So your agency wants my help as a psychic?"

He nodded. "I know you hate it, but you are a psychic, Georgette. And somehow Lily has reached you, or you've reached her. You led me to Crazy Eugene's this morning. That's all we're asking of you now—information if and when it comes to you. I can show you some pictures of Nilian rebels that are in New Orleans and of their leader, Ricardo Gonzalez. If the pictures and facts that I give you lead you to some kind of revelation, so be it. If they don't, we'll let it go."

Nothing had changed inside the panel truck, yet it seemed cramped where before it had seemed roomy and comfortable. The changes were coming too fast. The job she'd loved was on the line. Her boss was a depraved pervert who'd sold out to the enemy, and now a secret agency was seeking her help as a psychic, a label she hated with every fiber of her being.

"Where are the pictures?"

"I have them with me, but first you have to promise that all you'll do is tell me what you see in the visions. Under no circumstances will you do anything or confront anyone on your own."

"I'm not sure I can promise anything at this point."

"Then this is a no go. I won't have you putting yourself at risk."

She met Tanner's gaze and trembled. Whatever smouldered between them was intangible yet as real as the air they breathed. They were intricately bound by a deadly situation and the gift she longed to deny. And by some primal desire that took over at will.

"Okay. Show me what you've got."

SEBASTION TOSSED the hamburger patties onto the backyard grill, the routine for Sunday evenings. His wife was inside, mixing up a batch of brownies. His son was in the pool, splashing around with a couple of neighborhood friends. His daughter was curled up in one of the lounge chairs, reading one of the required books for her English class. Sebastion was amazed how much reading and homework was required of her in seventh grade, but she was in one of the best private schools money could buy.

Louise stepped through the back door, two drinks in hand. "Martinis for the cooks," she said, handing one of the drinks to him.

She was even more beautiful than on the day they'd married. She'd been a great catch. Socially prominent family. Rich. A graduate of Brown. Sweet and innocent. Good in bed, too, though nothing like the kind of sexual excitement he craved when the drug was in his system.

It was the drug that had changed him. If he could give it up, he'd be the same man he was before.

He watched as she sat on the edge of the pool and slipped her feet into the water. He wondered what she'd say if he showed her the pictures, wondered if there was a ghost of a chance she'd understand and forgive him, if she'd agree to just pack up and run so far Jerome Senegal could never touch any of them.

The answer came back at him and settled rock-hard in his gut. If he came out in the open, admitted that he'd been with the prostitutes, time after time after time, it would destroy her.

"Hey, Dad, come play pool basketball with us. We need you to even out the teams."

"Got to watch these burgers."

"I'll watch them," Louise said, standing and walking toward him, her short blond hair bouncing about her cheeks.

"That's a deal."

He dove into the pool for a game of basketball.

The perfect father. The perfect family. The perfect Sunday evening.

Seeing him now, who'd ever guess that he was about to play a role in sending his junior prosecutor on a journey and to a fate that would be a thousand times worse than death?

Chapter Twelve

"A scary troop of ruffians," Georgette commented, as Tanner brought up the last of the photographs and grouped them on the monitor. "I can believe they're wreaking havoc in their own country and on our streets as well, but I've never seen any of them before. I'm sure I would have noticed if they'd visited Sebastion at the office."

"What about psychic revelations? Do the pictures inspire anything?"

"A nebulous feeling of impending doom, but that could just be from the situation and the menacing appearance of the men themselves."

"It was worth a try," Tanner said.

"Exactly who are these men?"

"They're members of a group of insurgents from Nilia known as Scorpion Poison. They are all followers of an evil dictator called Black Death who is out to overthrow the current democratic government."

"I must confess that I don't know much about Nilia."

"It's a small country, militarily weak, but not poor. They're a major oil exporter."

"So Black Death stands to gain control over the oil money?"

"The oil money and the people. He's known for being a ruthless tyrant who doesn't hesitate to kill his own men. So it pretty much follows that he's going to kill a lot of the innocent citizens who oppose him now."

"Is Black Death in New Orleans?"

"No. Ricardo Gonzalez appears to be the leader of the rebel group who've infiltrated the city. The Scorpion Poison answers to him."

"So the black scorpion tattoo that was on the victim at Crazy Eugene's is their trademark, so to speak?"

"Right. The CIA alerted the government the rebels were in New Orleans a few months ago. Our assignment is to find out why they're here. So far we've discovered that they're involved with Jerome Senegal and we're almost certain they're shipping illegal drugs into the city and into Senegal's hands. Illegal drugs and coffee are the other exports they're known for."

"Is this a drug I'd be familiar with?"

"It's a new drug to this area, but you're familiar with some of its effects from recent incidents in the news. Right now, we just know it as Category Five."

"What's the addictive factor?"

"It's one of the most addictive we've seen in this country in quite a while. And even a small dose increases heart rate and sex drive to dangerous levels. Senegal's used it to trap and blackmail influential men like Sebastion and to lure rich, older tourists into his prostitution ring where he charges huge sums of money in exchange for their drug-induced sex craving.''

"How did you discover that?''

"One of our retired supervisors came to town and almost died from heart failure after having the drug slipped into his drink at a Bourbon Street nightclub.''

"Is he all right?''

"It was touch and go for a while, but he's recovering now.''

"If you know all that, why haven't you shut down Senegal's operations or provided the information to the police so that they can?''

"We've tried, even rushed the setup of our organization to get started earlier than scheduled. We found out that the drugs were being distributed through a local coffee company which served as a front. We took those out of operation. And we closed a very elite bordello that Senegal was operating in the Quarter. That slowed things down, but Senegal and Gaspard continue to find ways to keep his drug and prostitution business flowing.''

"Can't border control or FDA agents just seize the drugs either before or right after they're unloaded from the ships?''

"All the boats either coming from Nilia or having made a stop there before reaching our port have been searched. There is never any sign of the drug. For the most part the Nilia cargo ships docking in the New Orleans port have only delivered coffee.''

Georgette pushed her dark hair back from her face. The strain of all she'd been through was etched in tiny lines around her eyes and the grim, serious twist to her lips. Tanner hated that he'd had to lay all this on her.

"That's pretty much where we are," he said, hoping to leave it at that.

"Once the drugs are delivered, there would be no real reason for these tattooed guys to stick around," Georgette said. "So there has to be something more that you're not telling me."

"So you're not only a psychic, but smart," he said.

"Head of my class. So what's the real reason for having a secret agency involved in this instead of leaving it to the FDA? Are you concerned about some kind of terrorist threat from the Nilian rebels?"

"It's a possibility. Basically the Scorpion Poison hasn't broken any laws in our country that we know of, so none of the other agencies has a reason to deal with them. The CIA feels it's imperative to know exactly what their business is in this country. And that's how we got into the game."

"And with all this going on, you've still had to deal with Lily's disappearance."

He nodded. "Finding her necklace in a house with a murdered rebel hasn't helped."

Georgette left her chair, walked behind him and put her hands on his shoulders, digging her fingers into his taut muscles. "You loved Lily so much. Why did you never marry again and have more children?"

"Decided to quit while I was behind."

"You don't seem like a man who'd give up that easily."

"I'm smart enough to know my faults."

"Was Juliana the only woman you were ever in love with?"

"No. There was… You don't want to hear this, Georgette."

"I do if you want to talk about it."

"I don't." He couldn't. Not even now, years later. The pain had lessened over time. His memories of his first love had dimmed. But the knowledge that he'd failed her was seared into his brain forever. It had started a pattern he couldn't shake.

"What about you, Georgette? Why haven't you married?"

"I have too many people roaming around in my head to let a man move into my bed."

"The visions, you mean?"

"Right. The gift and a lasting relationship are pretty much mutually exclusive. And I have my career. Well, *had* my career."

She slid her hand down his chest and intertwined her fingers with his. "Let's not think of that now, Tanner. Let's concentrate on something we might be able to change. Hold my hands and we'll both pray hard for the images to appear and lead us to Lily."

Tanner prayed as best he knew how, more from the heart than the head. Prayed for the miracle that didn't come.

GEORGETTE ROLLED OVER, stared at the alarm clock by her bed and thought of Tanner. He was the last thing she'd thought about before falling asleep, and here she was at ten minutes after five thinking of him again. He was different from any man she'd ever known. Quiet, but determined. Self-assured yet never pushy or arrogant.

Lily was the bond that had brought Tanner into Georgette's life, yet she knew he was attracted to her. She saw it in his eyes when he looked at her, heard it in his voice. Mostly she felt it, an undercurrent that ran through every conversation they shared. She'd thought he'd kiss her good-night, but he'd only looked into her eyes and brushed the back of his hand across her cheek.

It was for the best. When this was over, she'd walk away no matter what had passed between them. If she didn't, the gift would eventually drive him away and that would be worse.

Her mind shifted to Sebastion, as opposite to Tanner as a man could be. He'd played both ends against the middle, shouting for tougher laws and longer jail sentences for criminals while being blackmailed and taking payoffs from the mob. She should have realized what was going on long ago. But he'd treated her like a protégée, and she'd trusted him completely.

The images in the photographs of him and the underage prostitutes flashed across her mind. How could he have done it? He was a family man. He took off work for his daughter's piano recital. He went camping with his son's Boy Scout troop. He'd helped his son with his science project.

The science project.

"Holy cripes!"

No wonder the paper that had fallen out of the folder that day looked far too complicated for a fourth-grade science project. She bounded out of bed and dove for the phone.

She punched in Tanner's number and waited five long rings for him to answer. When he did his voice was heavy with the dregs of sleep.

"Sorry to wake you," she said, "but this is important."

"What is it, Georgette? Are you all right?"

"I'm terrific, and I know why the rebels from Nilia are in New Orleans."

TANNER PULLED into an empty spot in Georgette's parking garage and slammed on the brakes. If she was right and she really had the answers they were looking for, Conrad Burke would want to sign her up on the spot.

He took the elevator to her floor and practically ran to her door, ignoring the sore, stiff muscles that still protested Friday night's beating.

She opened it at the first knock. He stepped inside, ready for the news, not ready for the sight of her in a pair of purple silk pajamas. The fabric hugged her hips and outlined the peaked tips of her nipples.

"I made coffee," she said, leading the way to the kitchen. He caught his breath on the way and tamped down the desire as much as he could.

"What does this look like to you?" she asked, tapping a drawing she'd laid out on the kitchen table."

"Some kind of missile, maybe ground-to-air. Where did you get this?"

"I sketched it a few minutes ago, but Sebastion had a drawing like that in a file on his desk Friday. Only his was a lot more detailed with numbers and figures all over it."

"He showed it to you?"

"No," she said as she poured two mugs of steaming coffee. "I went in to ask him a question and ended up knocking the folder off the corner of his desk. The papers scattered, and the one I picked up for him looked similar to this. I didn't get a good look at the others, but they appeared to be detailed drawings of machine guns and other weapons."

"Did he say why he had the file?"

"He said it was a science project he was working on with his son. His son's only in the fourth grade,

Tanner, and these were professional drawings. I forgot all about it until this morning when I was lying in bed thinking about Sebastion.''

"Missiles. Machine guns. Weapons to stock a rebel army.''

"And shoot down any planes that might come in to help the ruling party.''

"The Scorpion Poison in the States negotiating to buy arms, and Sebastion and Senegal are coordinating the arrangements. It computes,'' Tanner said. "This is big, Georgette. Really big.''

He grabbed her in a bear hug and spun her around the room. The movement was dizzying, the press of her breasts against him intoxicating.

Desire hit so strong, he felt as if he were about to explode. He set her feet back to the floor, but her arms stayed around his neck, and her lips were too close. Much too close.

She touched her mouth to his, and the kiss turned him inside out and back again. His hands splayed her back, then moved to her waist and dipped below the elastic of her pajama bottoms. The soft firm flesh melted into his hot hands. If he didn't stop now, he'd never be able to.

Not stop? Go all the way with Georgette Delacroix? What the devil was he thinking?

He jerked away. "Don't know what got into me,'' he muttered, his voice all hoarse and guttural.

"The excitement of the moment,'' she whispered. But her eyes were glazed with the smoky desire that had almost consumed them. And her lips were full and puffy from the fierce passion of the kiss.

He turned away, knowing if he didn't, he'd take her in his arms again and he didn't see how he could pull away a second time. "I need to call my boss and apprise him of the latest development. I'll need some privacy."

That came out all wrong, made it sound as if the kiss hadn't mattered at all, and it was only business he had on his mind. Or that he didn't trust her when she was the one who'd given him the information.

But then when had he ever said things right when his emotions got in the way?

"You can have the kitchen," she said. "I'll be in the bedroom, getting showered and dressed."

She walked to the door, then paused, as if she was waiting for something from him. Whatever it was she wanted, he didn't know how to give it. So he just punched in Burke's number, ready to go back to work, the one thing in life he knew how to handle.

TANNER FILLED Conrad Burke in on the possible arms deal and answered as many of his questions as he could.

"Smuggling illegally purchased weapons out of the country," Burke said. "That would explain it all. Drugs for guns."

"It's not the first time that's happened, and probably won't be the last."

"I don't plan for it to happen on the Confidential watch," Burke said. "I have some news as well. I heard from the Coast Guard about five minutes before your call. A cargo ship from Nilia is in the channel and will be making port in New Orleans sometime around noon or shortly thereafter."

"That doesn't give us much time to find out who's selling the weapons."

"Doesn't give us much time, period. I'm going to

call the other agents now and alert them as to the latest developments. I need some guys on the ground searching warehouses along the river for the rebels and the weapons and I'll want a couple of helicopters in the air, observing the boat and any unusual activity throughout the port area. Our main concern is stopping those weapons from leaving the country, but it would be a real bonus if we found out how they're sneaking those drugs into the country.''

"If it's okay with you, I'd like to man the surveillance vehicle today and then tail Sebastion when he leaves his office,'' Tanner said. "I'd like to catch him in the act of making payment on the arms deal.''

"You've earned that assignment. Do you want Bartley for backup?''

"No. Put him where you need him most, but tell him to be available. I'll call him if it looks like I need him.''

"Okay. Jeff's available. Use him as you see fit.''

"Will do.'' Jeff was the newest Confidential recruit, an ex navy Seal with lots of potential. Tanner trusted him a lot more than he trusted Mason Bartley.

"What about Georgette Delacroix?'' Burke asked.

"What about her?''

"Does she want to go with you?'' Burke asked.

"I'm sure she does, but it's out of the question.''

"She could be a help if she has more of those psychic visions that led you to Crazy Eugene's.''

"It's too dangerous.''

"It's your call, Tanner. Watch your back and stay alert. Looks like it's all going down today.''

Today. And what was going down were weapons, drugs, a major confrontation. But where was Lily in all of this? If ever he'd needed a psychic with a vision it was now. But he wouldn't drag Georgette into the danger.

He might have failed every woman who'd ever counted on him before. But not this time. Not Georgette.

MASON BARTLEY rubbed some aftershave on his hands, then patted it over his face, enjoying the astringent sting. Big day coming up. Burke wanted him on the streets scouring the warehouses along the riverfront, searching for any sign of the Hispanic blokes with their bulging tattooed muscles and chili-pepper breaths.

In town for what was probably their last day. He wondered how they'd spent their last night. Probably getting it on with some of Gaspard's high-class whores. Talk about an oxymoron.

Deciding his looks would pass, Bartley slipped his size-eleven dogs into a pair of Italian leather loafers and strode out the door, all revved up to be the first guy to wish the rebels bon voyage.

His phone rang before he got to his car. The caller ID didn't register. No surprise. He had friends in low places.

"Mason Bartley?"

"The one and only. What can I do for you?"

"Are you still looking for work?"

Sonofabitch. It was Jerome Senegal. "Yeah. I'm looking."

"Meet me on the levee just east of Nine Mile Point."

"How far east?"

"All depends. Just look for me."

"When?"

"Thirty minutes from right now."

"I don't know if I can get there that soon."

"Thirty minutes, if you want the work."

"See you there."

Well, what do you know? Turned out to be a lot bigger day than he'd expected. He was back in the real game.

LILY COWERED near the door of the tiny bathroom. There were no windows, no way to tell if it was day or night, rain or shine. She'd always been somewhat claustrophobic, and the condition had increased in severity from the second Tony had shoved her into this room. Her lungs burned continuously now and her breaths seemed void of oxygen.

Tony had brought her food and water once since she'd been here. The food was likely left over from his own meal—half a baked potato, a piece of cold fried chicken, a hunk of crusty French bread. Nothing had ever tasted better.

She'd stretched the bottle of water as far as she could, letting a small amount trickle down her dry throat at infrequent intervals. But it was gone now and she was so very, very thirsty.

The bathroom had running water, but when it ran, it looked like the spit of a man dipping snuff. She'd splashed some of it on her face, but she didn't dare drink it.

She could die of thirst right here, and Mum would never know what had happened to her. Neither would her dad. She'd dreamed last night that he'd busted right through the door, marched into the dirty bathroom and carried her to safety. But it was only a dream. He wasn't here now any more than he'd ever been there for her.

I needed you, Daddy. All those years. I needed you so badly.

Standing, she walked back to the stained basin and ran her index finger through the rusted sludge left by the discolored water. Then, using the gunk as ink, she smeared a message on the wall behind the door where it wouldn't be obvious if anyone stuck their head in to check on her.

Now if someone came looking for her, they would at least know she'd been here. But what chance was there anyone would search for her in a warehouse on the Mississippi River?

The only good thing was that her foot no longer throbbed. She hoped that was because Eugene's poultice had worked and not because it was rotting off or that she was merely numb to the pain.

She listened as the same scratching noise she'd been hearing for the last few hours or so started up again. It sounded as if someone were scooting things across the floor. There were voices again, too. Loud. And every sentence was punctuated with profanities and just plain filthy language. A rotten lot she was dealing with here in America.

The voices trailed off. Apparently they were leaving. Fear set in again. As much as she dreaded the thought that one of the men would open the door and force her to do things too terrible to think about, she was still afraid of being left here in this filthy bathroom to die.

After a while the scratching stopped. The constant whir of machinery had shut down now as well. The place was quiet—except for footsteps. They stopped outside her door and she saw the knob turn to the right. A second later the door squeaked open.

Tony stood there, his trousers and boxer shorts down around his ankles. She stared at them, refusing to look higher.

"Guess you're lonesome in here all by yourself."

"No."

"Hungry though, I'll bet. I brought you a treat."

Her stomach turned and her muddled mind struggled to find an escape from whatever he had in mind.

"I got breakfast waiting on you."

"Keep your breakfast."

"No need to get so uppity with me, you and that stuffy English accent. You worked for Gaspard just like the rest of those girls who'll do anything or anyone for a little cash."

"Well, I won't do you."

"We'll see about that." He grabbed her blouse and ripped it from her body. "Take off the bra and the panties."

"You want them off, you bloody well take them off yourself, you murdering SOB."

He leaned over to do it, and she planted two fingers in his eyes and jabbed as hard as she could. Screams tore from his throat as he stumbled backward, crashing into the wall.

She shoved past him and started running. All she had to do was get outside and to the street. Then surely someone would stop and help her. Her bare feet slapped against the cold cement floor stirring up a choking black dust that seemed to coat everything.

Her heart was pounding as she reached the door. Escape was in her grasp as she wrapped her hands around the doorknob and twisted with all her might.

She twisted again and again, only now tears were burning her eyes and running down her cheeks.

The door was locked. And when she turned around, Tony was striding toward her, the long jagged edge of a knife pointing right at her. There was no way to win. No way to escape the inevitable. The fight went out of her, and she crumpled to the floor.

She reached to her neck for the locket, then remembered even that was gone. Now there was only a man with a heart as black as night, and he was coming right at her.

"My father will make you pay for this."

"Before this day is over, your father will be dead. Now that I think about it, I may just hold off on killing you so that he can be there to watch you die. It will be a family reunion. Now, who said I'm not all heart?"

TANNER LOST the first phase of the argument, but he held tough on the most important element. He'd agreed that Georgette could hang out with him in the surveillance truck, but only after she promised she'd return home when he took off to follow Sebastion.

They'd started out at the D.A.'s office, then followed Sebastion to the courthouse for the 9:00 a.m. press conference covered by all the local radio and TV stations.

Tanner had parked where he could keep Sebastion's car in plain view while he and Georgette watched the proceedings on Channel Four. Burke had attended the conference and kept an eye on Sebastion to make certain he didn't leave by a back exit or in a vehicle other than his own.

He hadn't, and the conference had gone as expected, except that the usually unflappable district attorney had seemed distracted and nervous, twice asking a reporter to repeat his question.

Now Tanner and Georgette were back in their parking spot near Georgette's office, impatiently waiting and monitoring Sebastion's every move.

"At least destroying my professional reputation seemed to upset him," Georgette said, watching as Sebastion shook a couple of antacid tablets from the bottle in his top drawer and swallowed them whole.

"Something is bothering him," Tanner agreed. "Who's the young man who just walked into his office?"

"Mark Efram. He's a law student from Tulane who's doing an internship with us."

Mark asked his question, then left. Sebastion's phone rang and thanks to the wiretap, they listened to both sides of the conversation.

"How did I do?" Sebastion asked as soon as his wife said hello.

"You did fine, sweetheart."

"Guess you could tell I was nervous."

"Some. This thing with Tony Arsenault is really getting to you."

"Don't worry about me. I'll be fine. What about you? What do you have planned for the rest of the day?"

"I have a Junior League meeting at lunch, and I have to drive Rebecca to piano lessons after school. After that, I'm free. Will you be home for dinner?"

"Don't count on it. I may be working late."

"Not again."

"Sorry, sweetheart."

"Okay. Give me a call later."

"Sure. I know I don't say this often enough, but I just want you to know that you and the kids mean everything to me."

"You sound so serious, Sebastion. Are you sure you're okay?"

"Nothing wrong with a man telling his wife he loves her, is there?"

"No. Tell me any time. Take care. I'll see you tonight."

And that was it. Tanner settled back in his chair. He was impatient and edgy himself, ready to get the show on the road.

Georgette swiveled her chair around to face him. "What did you think of the phone call?"

"Routine. Why?"

"I got this really strange feeling when they were talking, as if Sebastion thought he might never see his wife again. It gave me the creeps."

"Something psychic?"

"I don't know. I'm never sure how much of what I feel is normal intuitive reactions and how much is extrasensory phenomena."

She hugged her arms about her chest, and Tanner could almost feel her pulling away from him and back into herself. The moment became awkward. He understood so little of what she referred to as the gift that he couldn't even ask sensible questions.

Or maybe it was just awkward because the kiss sat between them now. It verified the desire that burned just beneath the surface of their fragile relationship, but didn't justify it.

He wasn't sure what would.

Sebastion's phone rang again. Both he and Georgette jerked to attention as the voice on the other end of the line spoke one sentence and then hung up. "Corner of Ursulines and Decatur. Now."

"This is it," Tanner said. "Go straight home, Georgette. Lock your doors and stay there. I'll call you when I can."

She put her arms around him and they both held on tight.

"Be careful, Tanner. Please be careful."

He nodded and put his finger to her lips before she said more. The adrenaline was flowing and he had a job to do. He couldn't let emotion of any kind get to him now.

Only it did. Not that he could name it, but something cold and frightening wrapped around his heart as she squeezed his hand one last time before opening the door and walking away.

He grabbed the mike for the two-way radio and issued an order to Jeff. "She's heading for her car. Make sure she gets home safely."

That was all there was time for. The race to stop the arms deal was on.

Chapter Thirteen

Tanner found a parking spot a half block away, close enough to see what was going on, and, he hoped, far enough away that he wouldn't be noticed.

Sebastion arrived a few minutes later by taxi. It was a fairly busy corner on the edge of the French Quarter, only a couple of blocks from where Tanner had found the beaten and bleeding prostitute.

Tanner got out of the white panel truck and ducked under an overhanging balcony in front of an antique shop. The angle gave him a better view. Reaching in his shirt pocket, he pulled out the sunglasses that gave him binocular vision.

If Jerome Senegal and Sebastion faced him while they were talking, he'd probably be able to read their lips well enough to pick up some of the conversation and perhaps see where they were off to next. Tanner doubted the deal would actually go down here.

Someone walked up and put a hand on his elbow. He jerked around, one hand flying to the butt of the gun he had hidden inside the camera case strapped about his waist.

But it was only a working girl. She looked familiar, and way too young to be soliciting. No doubt one of

Gaspard's underage recruits. "Peddle somewhere else," he snapped, his gaze returning to Sebastion. "I'm not interested."

"I think you are."

"No. I'm not."

"I know where Lily is."

His heart knotted, and he jerked her in front of him so that he could watch both her and Sebastion. "Who put you up to this?"

"No one. I saw you when you came to the party looking for Lily. I know where she is."

He knew now why she looked familiar. She'd been on the balcony talking to Maurice Gaspard when he'd walked up. He was being set up. He was *almost* sure of it. "Why are you telling me this?"

She glanced over her shoulder then back at him. "They're going to kill her 'cause she saw some knife guy whack a couple of people."

"Tony the Knife?"

"I told you what I know."

A black car pulled up and stopped at the corner. Sebastion walked over, opened the back door and slid inside. If Tanner didn't jump in his vehicle now, he'd lose the tail.

"Come with me," he said, dragging Becky along. "And hurry."

She grabbed hold of a parking meter and stood her ground. "Let go of me. I'll be in big trouble if they see me with you."

A couple of camera-toting tourists with Mardi Gras beads dangling from their necks stopped to stare at him tugging on the young woman. Cops would show up soon. And Sebastion would be too far out of sight to follow.

"Please go with me," he pleaded.

"Go where?"

"To find Lily. And don't worry about Gaspard. I won't let him hurt you. I promise."

She let go of the parking meter and let him lead her to the truck. He jerked the gear into Reverse, bumping the car behind him and leaving a little rubber behind as he revved the engine and took off after the black car.

"Now tell me where Lily is."

"She's in a warehouse on the river. The knife guy is there refining drugs so they can sell them."

"How do you know this?"

"I sneak around, and I listen."

This had all the markings of a setup, but he half believed her. And half was more than enough reason to check out her story. He called his partner Mason Bartley on his cell phone. "I've got a lead on Lily," he said, "and I'm tailing Sebastion to what may be final negotiation and payment on the arms deal. Can you check out the lead for me?"

"Sure, if you want. But why don't I do the tailing and you go after your daughter? You know what you're looking for."

Made sense. Plus Tanner had the lead with him. "Where are you?"

"Just coming down from the Crescent City Connection, taking the Okeefe exit."

"I'm on Esplanade, heading toward Rampart. Sebastion's a block in front of me, a passenger in a black, late-model Lexus."

"Tags?"

Tanner gave him the license number, then sped through a yellow light so as not to get left behind.

Five minutes later, Mason waved and passed Sebastion. "Go get your daughter, Dad."

"Thanks." Tanner broke the connection, hating to give the job to Bartley, but knowing he couldn't do both tasks.

"Wow. This is fun. Just like being in an action movie."

Tanner turned back to the girl. "Do you have a name?"

"Becky Lane."

"Okay, Becky. We're going after Lily. Tell me everything you know."

"I already did. She's in that warehouse, locked in a bathroom."

"What warehouse?"

"You mean there's more than one?"

He groaned. He should have known this was too good to be true.

A LONG, HEARTBREAKING HOUR and a half dozen warehouses later, Tanner gave Becky a hundred-dollar bill and told her to check into a hotel on Airline Highway until he called and told her it was safe to go back out on the streets. He doubted she'd follow his orders, but he couldn't very well lock her up for trying to help him.

He'd scouted out every inch of the warehouse area since he'd signed on with New Orleans Confidential. He knew it like the back of his hand, maybe better, the port area was so vital to their investigation.

There weren't a lot more places to search for Lily, and what was left were unlikely locations for Senegal to be using to refine drugs. There was one, though, out on River Road. A rambling place that didn't appear to have been used as anything but a giant rat trap for years. Still, he'd try it, kind of a last-ditch effort before he admitted he'd been had.

He called Bartley on his way to the warehouse. No answer. That could mean anything. He hoped it meant he was meeting with success. He tried to get Burke. No answer there, either. He settled for Burke's wife. Not that talking to Marilyn was actually settling. She'd been working on a case with Colorado Confidential when she'd fallen for Conrad. After that investigation ended, she traded in her high-powered career for a part-time management position at Crescent City Transports so she could devote the majority of her time to raising their beloved twins.

"Conrad's at the ship, monitoring the activity. I'm not sure who's there with him, but I know the customs officers cleared it for unloading."

"Where's it docked?"

She gave him the location. "I haven't heard anything in the last half hour."

"No word probably means they're not loading the arms yet. That could be a good sign."

"Or it could mean the rebels are outsmarting us with the arms the way they've done with the drugs. For all we know, while we're checking the obvious boat, they're loading guns onto a tanker flying the flag of some country we would never suspect."

"You can bet Burke's checking that out as well."

"No one can be everywhere. You know that." She sighed. "Don't mind me. I'm just going crazy because I'm missing out on the action—and worried about Conrad. What's the news on Lily? Bartley told Burke you had a sound lead."

"It's disintegrating as we speak." He filled her in

on the details, knowing he sounded the way he felt, like a pathetic failure.

He finished the conversation and turned off the Westbank Expressway at Baritaria Boulevard and headed back to the river. Strange thing about the Westbank. It was on the east bank of the Mississippi River. But when you crossed the river, you were going west. It was just the crescent bend in the river that made things confusing.

There wasn't a car in sight when he pulled in beside the old warehouse. He parked near the street entrance. The place was deserted as he'd expected, but there was a stack of trash outside the building. It contained packing materials, a fast food chicken sack and an empty donut box.

The trash hadn't been there long. The wind would have blown it away if it had been. Hope skidded along his nerve endings as he jogged to the door. He didn't bother with finesse, just took out his pistol and shot the lock off.

The pungent odor of coffee beans hit his nostrils the second the door squeaked open. A heavy black dust floated on the air and clogged in his lungs as he stepped inside and took a quick look around.

Someone had been here recently. There were footprints in the black residue.

"Lily!"

He called her name, then listened. When there was no response he started checking out the building, moving slowly, gun in hand and finger on the trigger in case this was a trap.

He opened a couple of doors but didn't have to spend much time examining the rooms. They were mostly empty except for a couple of old desks and rusty file cabinets. One held an old refrigerator with the door removed.

Locked in a bathroom. Becky's words played in his mind as he checked out a room with one stall and a urinal falling out of a crumbling wall. No sign of Lily.

There was one last door, all the way across the big empty space. He hurried toward it and pushed the door open. Another empty bathroom. He kicked the door so hard it rattled the hinges and knocked a hole in the plaster. He'd give anything to have his hands around Gaspard's neck right now.

No. It was Tony Arsenault he wanted. If Becky was right, this had started with Lily's seeing him make a hit. Tanner stepped backward, and that's when he spotted the message that had been smeared across the wall.

Help me, Daddy. Love, Lily.

The weight of the world crashed into his chest, crushing what was left of his heart. His daughter had been here, begging for his help. He'd come to save her, but he'd come too late.

GEORGETTE STRIPPED the sheets from the bed and carried them to the laundry room. She'd been cleaning the condo all day, though the cleaning woman had been there only four days ago. But she needed something physical to burn up her restless energy.

She poured in a capful of liquid detergent and set the temperature to hot. Once the machine was filling with water, she pulled the phone from her pocket and checked again to make sure it was on.

If Tanner would only call and let her know he was all right, she'd be able to settle down, or at least quit bouncing off the walls. She started back to the bedroom to put on the clean sheets, but stopped in her tracks.

Shudders shook her body. Something was wrong. Something was dreadfully wrong. There was no trance. There were no images. But cold, crippling fear raced through her bloodstream.

The phone rang. She reached for it, but it fell from her trembling fingers and clattered about on the polished hardwood floors. Stooping, she retrieved it and answered.

"Hello, Georgette."

"Who is this?"

"I'm calling for Tanner."

"Is this his partner?"

"Yes. I'm his partner."

"Tanner's hurt, isn't he?" He was injured and that's why the fear had attacked so fiercely and without warning.

"Yes. He's hurt."

"But not dead? Please tell me he's not dead."

"He's not dead, but he's seriously injured and he's asking for you. Will you come?"

"Yes. Yes, of course, I'll come. Where is he?"

"I can't tell you that, but I can take you to him. Meet me outside your condominium in ten minutes. Is that too soon?"

"I'll be there."

If she hadn't known before how much she cared for Tanner, she knew now. She didn't know if what she felt was love, but the intensity of the emotions he stirred in her was almost too much to bear.

ISABELLA DELACROIX stared at the deck of tarot cards spread out in front of her. Her client had paid good money to hear what she had to say, but the woman only half believed her and her doubts were getting in the way of Isabella's concentration.

"I can only tell what the cards say. I'm not responsible for the message. You were the one who picked them."

"Then forget the cards. Just tell me if my husband is running around on me. That's all I came to find out anyway."

The answer was yes, but it didn't take a psychic to figure it out. It was written all over her face.

But she didn't want to know and that's why she was here. She wanted Isabella to convince her that her husband was faithful. Isabella never lied, but she was frequently guilty of coloring the truth in comforting pastels.

"Your husband...your husband..."

"What about him?"

Isabella's hand flew over the cards, sending them scattering to the floor. They were bloody and the images on them were twisting into grotesque black scorpions. All except one. It was still on the table staring at her. It was the face of horror.

"What's wrong?" the woman asked, her voice grinding its way into Isabella's state of semiconsciousness. "What has my husband done?"

"It's not your husband. It's my daughter. She's being carried onto a floating hell."

Chapter Fourteen

"Speak up or forever hold your peace."

"If I had some peace, Bartley, I'd hold it."

"Tanner. Where are you, man? Did you find Lily?"

"I found where she's been. She's not there now, and I've run smack into another brick wall."

"Same here."

"What does that mean?"

"I lost the tail on the D.A.."

"Tell me you're joking."

"Don't I wish? The guy was switching lanes like a deranged Nascar driver. I had him in sight, though, until some babe in one of those monster SUVs pulled right in front of me and slowed down. By the time I got around her, the car with Sebastion was long gone."

"You must have done something to tip him off he was being followed."

"Uh-uh. I know how to tail a car. Been knowing that since I was big enough to see over a steering wheel."

"Then maybe you got confused this time about which side you're on."

''Go right ahead and take your frustration out on me if it helps. But you're beating a dead dog with that suspicion crap.''

Tanner hung up the phone before he said something he might regret later. He hadn't trusted Mason Bartley from the get-go. Ex-cons never went totally straight. It was a fact of life.

Tanner parked the truck near Sebastion's office, though he didn't see much reason to ride herd on the man after the fact. He crawled into the back of the van, flicked on the equipment, then took out his phone and called Georgette.

He didn't expect any good news from her, either. If she'd received new psychic input about Lily's whereabouts, she'd have called him. But bad as he hated to admit it, he just plain needed to hear her voice.

The phone rang repeatedly before it clicked and informed him that Georgette Delacroix was unavailable and that he could leave a message at the sound of the tone. Probably in the shower, he decided, or maybe gone for a dip in the complex's pool. He'd have heard from Jeff if she hadn't made it home safely.

Still, the situation made him uneasy. He called her back and left a message to get in touch with him, then adjusted the temperature on the air-conditioning controls. The day was already a scorcher and on its way to getting a lot hotter.

He stood in front of the vent and let a blast of cool air dry the perspiration from his shirt, but turned to face the monitor when the audio bug in Sebastion's office clicked on.

He watched as Sebastion shut and locked his office door, then walked to his desk and collapsed in his chair. His hands shook like those of a man in detox as he picked up the phone and punched in a series of numbers.

Jerome Senegal answered on the second ring.

"Where's Georgette?" Sebastion asked, not bothering to say hello.

"Where I told you she'd be."

"No reason for that. All she did was ask about Tanner one time. She doesn't know anything."

"Don't be so stupid. She's in this to her eyeballs. Why else would she have been with him down the bayou Friday night? My guy should have killed her then. He knows that now, too."

"I'm begging, Jerome. Don't do this to Georgette. It's inhuman."

"Stop wasting your breath. The deal is done. She's on the ship, entertainment for the lonesome rebels on their long voyage home."

Tanner didn't wait to hear more.

TANNER FORCED HIMSELF to think only of his course of action on his breakneck drive to the spot where the Nilian ship was docked. Any other kind of thoughts would drive him mad.

He considered calling Burke for backup, but decided this would go better as a one-man operation. If Gonzalez noticed anything suspicious, he'd likely kill Georgette on the spot.

Besides, Tanner didn't want to be the reason for Burke showing his hand too soon. The boss would play the game smart, wait until the arms were actually loaded on the ship and it was ready to sail before making a move.

That way they had an open-and-shut case against Gonzalez and his motley band of rebels, and Confidential and the Coast Guard would be assured of seizing all the artillery and ammunition involved in the deal. Once Gonzalez realized what was coming down, all hell would probably break loose. Tanner had to have Georgette off the ship before then.

He parked a block away in a crowded parking lot to lessen the chance that Burke or one of the other Confidential agents would notice his arrival and wonder what the hell he was up to. Now all he had to do was look the part of a longshoreman just doing his job.

His jeans were old and worn. They'd do fine. The shirt didn't quite make the cut. He yanked it off and wadded it into a tight ball, producing enough wrinkles to give it that worked-in look. For good measure, he dug a used coffee cup from the trash can and smeared the few drops of leftover coffee down the front of the shirt.

Turning, he checked his reflection in a small mirror mounted above one of the monitors. His face was still bruised, his eye ringed in shades of blues and purples. An added bonus, he decided. People would be less likely to mess with him if he looked like a barroom brawler.

He raked his hair back from his face, then grabbed the LSU cap that Jeff had left in the truck last week. "Go, Tigers," he quipped, tossing the hat to the floor. He stamped on it a few times, then stuck it on his head backward.

Ready or not, he was boarding ship.

He walked at a near jog, working up a good sweat. The vessel was small in comparison to a lot of the cargo carriers that traveled in and out of the busy New Orleans port, but it no doubt had plenty of places to hide a prisoner.

Lots of ship. Limited time.

Doubts surfaced, settling in Tanner's stomach like acid spilling onto raw flesh. His failure to protect the women in his life was legendary. His successes few.

But the consequences of a fouled operation were unthinkable. This time, failure was not at option.

RICARDO GONZALEZ took a long, satisfying drag on the Cuban cigar. Success was sweet. Black Death would surely make him a general when he returned to Nilia with an arsenal of high-tech weapons and the ammunition to go with them. And once they were in command of the country, Gonzalez would be a member of the ruling class. He'd live in a mansion. Drink the finest wine. Have women like those who worked for Maurice Gaspard every night of his life if he wanted them—and he'd have the beautiful Georgette Delacroix for his own.

The weapons were being loaded now, right under the noses of U.S. customs officials. The plan was ingenious and foolproof, the same as the drug imports had been. Ricardo Gonzalez was simply too smart for the Americans.

Once they were on the open water, he'd call for Georgette. She'd fuss and try to fight him off—part of the game women like her played. He did love a sassy woman.

He was so lost in his fantasies, he almost didn't

see the longshoreman ducking into a stairwell where he had no business.

"You! Halt!"

The guy took off running. Gonzalez took off after him, but stopped when six of the ship's crewmen stepped out of the engine room and right into the man's path.

Gonzalez shouted orders in Spanish, and two of the crewmen grabbed the man. The longshoreman looked familiar, but it wasn't until Gonzalez was only a step away that he connected him with the photograph Jerome Senegal had shown him just yesterday.

"Welcome aboard, Tanner Harrison. Were you looking for me? Or did you just join the party so you can watch your girlfriend and I in action?"

Tanner spat at him. The saliva hit Gonzalez in the forehead and rolled down his face. He made a fist and reared back, ready to smash it into Tanner's face.

He changed his mind when he noticed something on the floor at his feet. He picked up the woven scrap and waved it in Tanner's face.

Tanner landed a knee to Gonzalez's crotch. The pain was excruciating. Gonzalez growled a stream of curses in Spanish while one of the crewmen planted a fist in Tanner's face.

"Hold his mouth open," Gonzalez ordered. When they did, Gonzalez stuffed the scrap down the back of Tanner's throat. He smirked as Tanner began to choke and laughed out loud as the woven drug began to dissolve and trickle down his throat.

The unprocessed drug was much stronger than the product Senegal sold on the street. In a matter of minutes, Tanner's heart would simply beat itself to death.

"Search him for a weapon, take his cell phone and then throw him in the hold with the American woman," Gonzalez ordered. "Let her watch him die."

GEORGETTE OPENED her eyes as the door to the small room opened and Tanner was shoved inside. One of the crewmen muttered something in Spanish, and the other laughed boisterously before slamming the door shut again, locking it from the outside with the thick metal latch.

Tanner looked right at her, but didn't seem to see her. His eyes were glazed, his pupils enlarged. She hurried to his side to help support him, but he staggered backward, then lapsed into a wheezing spasm and fell against the wall.

"What's wrong, Tanner? What did they do to you?"

His only answer was a beastly gurgling sound at the back of his throat. His eyes bulged, and his bruised face turned an even darker shade of bluish gray.

Oh, no! He was choking. Something had to be stuck in his windpipe.

Frantic, Georgette got behind him and circled him with her arms, fitting her hands in the sternum area. She'd seen countless posters on how to administer the Heimlich maneuver, but everything about it seemed hazy now.

Fortunately, Tanner didn't wait to be saved. He reached down his own throat and yanked out what appeared to be a greenish piece of burlap.

He panted for breath, then slid down the wall to sit

on the floor. "The...drug..." he muttered, his words almost swallowed in his spiky gasps for air.

She sat beside him. "They drugged you?" she asked, trying to grasp his meaning.

"No." He kicked at the scrap of cloth that he'd torn from his throat. "This is...the drug...disguised."

"That piece of burlap is what the Nilian rebels have been smuggling into the country?"

He nodded. "Held...coffee."

Finally, it sank in. The raw form of the drug had been woven into fabric, then made into bags that held the imported coffee beans. The mob used their secret drug labs to process the unrefined material into powdered drugs that were being distributed on the street.

"Heart is...racing."

Georgette lay her cheek against Tanner's chest and both felt and heard the erratic hammering. This was the same drug that had resulted in several tourist deaths. Those were mere overdoses. There was no way to know how much of the raw drug Tanner had ingested, except that it couldn't have been in his throat long. He would have choked to death.

"Came to...save you... Failed. Always fail."

She held him in her arms and rocked him back and forth as tears streamed down her cheeks. "Oh, Tanner. You didn't fail. You came. You're my hero."

"Failed you...failed Lily."

"Don't talk this way. Please don't talk this way." He needed help and he needed it now. She jumped up and beat on the door with both her fists. Someone had to hear. Someone had to help them.

But no one came. Finally she sank back to the floor and sat beside him.

"You're beau...beau-ti-ful." He caressed one of her breasts with his shaking hands.

Her mouth flew open. How could he possibly be thinking of sex at a time like this?

The drug, of course. Enhancing sexual desire was a major side effect.

Hard shudders shook his body as the drug infiltrated his system, shutting it down. He could die. And if he did— If he did, she'd be used to pleasure Gonzalez as he saw fit. She retched, then picked up the piece of burlap and slipped it into her pocket. If it came to that, she'd take the drug herself. She'd take death.

But she wasn't giving up yet. Not by a long shot.

"Should have...made...love," Tanner muttered between shudders.

"You're right. We should have made love."

"WHERE THE DEVIL is Tanner?" Conrad Burke demanded, once he and his agents had gathered for an impromptu meeting at the helicopter pad. "He'll be fit to be tied if he misses the action."

"I hope he's chasing a successful lead on his daughter," Mason said. "The guy deserves a break."

"Speaking of action," Seth Lewis said, "the vessel's churning out of sight as we speak, so what's the plan?"

"The weapons are definitely on board," Burke said. "Enough firepower to take out a small country— hor a city the size of New Orleans. The Coast Guard officials and I agree that Gonzalez and his group are crazy enough that they just might blow it all up rather than have us confiscate it. So we've decided it's safer if the confrontation takes place in the shipping channel outside the city.''

''Do we know how the weapons are packaged?'' Alexander McMullin asked.

''Inside the casings of medical equipment and sandwiched in-between legal drugs and other medical supplies. Lewis and I discovered the method using the portable and very powerful X-ray machines developed specifically for Confidential operations.''

''So is the Coast Guard running the show from here on out, or are we in charge?'' Bartley asked.

''It's the Coast Guard's game. We don't exist, remember? But we'll be there. I'll be on the Coast Guard ship. The rest of you will be in helicopters, overseeing the operation and ready to help if needed. Basically, we've done what we were established to do. Found out why the Scorpion Poison was hanging out in New Orleans and set it up for the Coast Guard to shut down their operation. A job well done, guys. I couldn't be prouder. Of course, it took a spunky female attorney to show us the way.''

''Can't wait to meet Ms. Delacroix,'' Bartley agreed, ''but I'd still like to know how they're smuggling the dope in.''

''And would I ever like to put Jerome Senegal and Maurice Gaspard behind bars,'' Lewis added.

''Include Sebastion Primeaux in the mix, and I'll second that,'' Burke said. ''Now I suggest you get into wet suits, just in case some of you decide to go to the aid of an overboard or escaping Nilian. And I'd still like to know what happened to Tanner Harrison.''

''Don't look at me,'' Bartley said. ''My partner doesn't tell me anything.''

LOUISE PRIMEAUX squirmed in her chair and tried to focus on the speaker, but hearing about the plans for this year's major fund-raiser couldn't hold her interest. She'd hoped Sebastion would settle into the daily routine once the press conference was behind him, but when she'd called him a few minutes ago, he'd seemed more distraught than ever.

She knew he hated putting Georgette on suspension, but it was having Tony Arsenault back on the street that was really getting to him. He loved being district attorney. And he was the man for the job, dedicated to making the city safe. But he couldn't do it by himself, and the effort wasn't worth his mental and physical health.

The speaker sat down and the group of well-heeled women applauded enthusiastically. Louise picked up her handbag and slipped out the back door. She was probably overreacting, but she couldn't get Sebastion off her mind.

The hotel where the luncheon meeting was being held was only a few blocks from Sebastion's office. She'd stop by and surprise him, maybe even talk him into coming home early to go skinny-dipping in the pool and enjoy a little afternoon delight before the kids got out of school.

She smiled at the thought. Nice to still be in love after nearly sixteen years of marriage. But why shouldn't she be? Sebastion was a terrific husband.

SEBASTION STARED OUT the window, looking over the city of New Orleans. *His* city. He'd grown up here, not in the ritzy neighborhood where he lived now, but in a little house out in the Gentilly area. His father had been a cop, his mother a teacher. They'd had values and standards. They were probably rolling over in their graves now.

This had all started when someone had slipped the powdered drug into Sebastion's drink at a political fund-raiser for Judge Boutte. Sebastion had ended up at Gaspard's bordello that night with a bevy of underage prostitutes. He barely remembered it, but the whole show had been captured on video.

He should have admitted it all then, explained what had happened and begged Louise to forgive him. But he hadn't wanted to lose his job. Nor had he wanted to stop. He'd gone back again and again, craved the drug and the sex. Now Jerome Senegal owned his soul.

And there was no way out—but one.

He unzipped his briefcase and took out the small pistol he'd put in there just this morning. If he were dead, the blackmail would be over. His wife and family would be safe. Even Senegal wouldn't go after a dead man's family. It was an unnecessary risk, simply bad business.

And Sebastion wouldn't have to face himself every day knowing that he'd helped put killers on the street, supplied arms to a tyrant and sold an innocent attorney into sexual slavery. All he had to do was pull the trigger. It would be a better ending than he deserved.

TANNER OPENED his eyes and looked around, wondering where he was. Then it all came back to him. The ship. The drug. Georgette. He had to get her out of here. But… "The ship is moving."

"Tanner. You're talking."

"Yeah. Guess I passed out there for a few minutes."

"More than a few."

"It was the drug." He put his right hand over his heart. "It's still beating too fast."

"Not like it was," she said.

Her face was red and her eyes were swollen. She'd been crying. "You okay?" he asked.

"I'm better now. But we have to get off this ship."

"Great idea. So how do you propose we do that?"

"Call your agency. Tell them to save us."

He looked around. "Cheap ship. Doesn't even have a phone in our room. And smoke signals would be a little dangerous on a vessel loaded with ammunition."

"Then we'll have to find a way to escape this room and jump ship. The river's not that wide. We could make it to shore."

"It's not wide, but the undertow is treacherous. And if they spot us, they'll shoot us." He stood and walked to the door, shook it and heard the rattle of the metal latch.

He looked back to Georgette. Crazy, but he was thinking more about how enticing her breasts were than he was of escaping. He wondered if her panties were lacy or plain, and if the triangle of hair at the apex of her thighs was as dark and shiny as the hair on her head.

He tugged on his jeans. His member was pushing so hard against them, it might break right through the fabric if he didn't let it out. He slid the zipper down for a little relief and thought about throwing Georgette to the floor and taking her right here and now.

"Why are you unzipping your jeans?"

He figured that was pretty obvious, but didn't want to say he was fighting an almost overpowering urge to jump her bones. "Just need a little relief," he said, breathing heavy.

She stared at his crotch. "The drug has got you going again."

Of course. This was the drug talking through his libido. "Powerful stuff. Category Five." He put his arms around her waist.

She backed away from him. "No, Tanner, not like this. I don't want our first time to be on a ship heading to Nilia, and I want it to be more than a reaction to a drug."

"What if we skip the first time and go straight to the second?"

"No. Forget sex. Concentrate on our predicament. We have to get off this ship before it reaches the Gulf."

"Okay, give me a minute."

The minute passed. The urges didn't. But he knew Georgette was right. They escaped soon or they didn't escape at all. Unfortunately he didn't have a clue how they were going to do that.

GONZALEZ STOOD on deck watching the scenery pass, anxious to get out of the shipping channels and into the Gulf of Mexico. Not that he expected any trouble from American authorities at this late hour, but he'd still feel better when they could open up the engines and increase their speed.

It would be so nice to be home again.

"The captain wants you to come to the control deck, sir. It's urgent."

Gonzalez jumped, startled by the young crewman who'd walked up behind him. "Did the captain say what this is about?"

"We received a radio message from the U.S. Coast Guard. They want us to stop so that they can come aboard."

"That's ridiculous. We've cleared customs. Everything on this ship is in order."

The Coast Guard couldn't have found out about the smuggled artillery. Maybe they just wanted to warn them of bad weather in the Gulf or perhaps an oil spill. The Americans worried about everything.

He turned at the sound of approaching choppers. Six of them. And there were three large Coast Guard boats all but blocking the channel in front of them.

Gonzalez shoved the crewman out of his way and took off, hitting the control room at a dead run.

"We repeat. This will be a peaceful takeover unless you resist."

Gonzalez yanked the radio mike from the ship's captain. "We've broken no law."

"We have evidence that you have smuggled goods on board. If this is in error, you'll be allowed to proceed. If not, we'll take over the ship and return it to port."

They knew. They couldn't, but they did. They would come on board. They'd take the arms off the ship. They might even put him in jail, but if they didn't, he'd have to return to Nilia without the money or the weapons.

He'd be ridiculed. Maybe even tortured. Or shot.

But there was no way for one small ship to take on the U.S. Coast Guard.

"Request to come aboard granted," he said, making an instant decision.

"Have your crew line the deck, hands in the air,

no weapons. And we want Ricardo Gonzalez in plain sight.''

''Take over,'' Gonzalez said to the ship's captain. ''Get the crew on deck.''

''They want you out there, too.''

''Right.'' But he wouldn't be there, and he wouldn't give up the arms. He'd go down, but he'd go down in a flame of glory and take everyone and everything on board the ship down with him.

Via La Rebellion.

Chapter Fifteen

Georgette grabbed Tanner's arm. "Do you feel that? I think the ship is stopping."

"It is." He just wasn't sure what it meant.

Static blared from the speaker system, followed by a crackled announcement in Spanish.

"He said something about the Coast Guard," Georgette said, her dark eyes dancing, "but I couldn't understand the rest of it. Do you speak Spanish?"

"Enough. The captain announced that the Coast Guard is in the immediate area and that they're coming aboard. He ordered the crew to the deck."

"Yes!" Georgette squealed, jumping in the air and doing a couple of cheerleader moves that Tanner didn't need to see in his present state of arousal. He fought the untimely urges and concentrated on the situation. If the arms were on board, and he had to assume they were, then the Coast Guard could well be about to seize the boat.

The perfect solution for Georgette and him. Only it sounded much too easy. He never trusted easy.

Georgette raced past him and started beating on the door. "Let us out!" she screamed. "The U.S. Coast Guard is here to save us. Let us out!"

Amazingly, someone who looked as if he'd been swabbing toilets opened the door, shouted something at them in Spanish and walked off. Tanner grabbed Georgette's hand and led her to the nearest stairwell. Adrenaline surged through him, apparently warding off enough of the aftereffects of Category Five that he was reasonably functional.

One deck up, he got his first whiff of smoke. One more deck and he was certain something was burning. If the flames ignited the ammunition, the vessel would become a ball of fire. No one would get off alive. So much for easy.

Tanner began to run, pulling Georgette along with him, not slowing for breath until they reached the open deck. He searched quickly for a life jacket, then noticed a stash of them in a wooden crate a few steps from the stairwell.

He grabbed one and pushed it into Georgette's arms. "Put this on and belt it around you," he ordered. "Then run to the railing and jump overboard. Don't hesitate and don't let anyone stop you. Just jump and then swim away from the boat as far and as fast as you can."

She flashed him a when-did-you-lose-your-mind? look. "I'm not jumping."

"Don't argue. There's no time."

"Look," she said, pointing. "Not one but three Coast Guard boats. And helicopters. We don't have to jump. They'll get us off this boat."

"Not quickly enough. Put your arms through here." He pulled the life jacket around her and fastened it himself. "Now hit the water."

"Be reasonable, Tanner."

"I am reasonable. Do you smell the smoke? Did you forget what's loaded on the cargo deck?"

Terror widened her eyes. "I'm not jumping without you, Tanner."

Nice sentiment. Bad timing. "Jump. I'll meet you later. That's a promise." He held her close for one heartbreaking second, then gave her a shove and took off toward what he hoped was the control tower.

Gonzalez had likely set the fire himself. Which meant he had chosen to let the crew and his followers be blown away.

The scorpion had a deadly sting.

GEORGETTE STOOD on the port side of the ship and stared into the choppy river below. It was a long jump into deep, murky water. She swung one leg over the railing, then looked around for Tanner. He was nowhere in sight. A group of crewmen stood a few yards away, yelling at her in Spanish.

She heard a splash. She didn't see anything, but it could have been Tanner. He might already be in the water waiting for her. The seamen were still yelling at her, and two of them were rushing toward her.

She threw her other leg over the railing, held her nose and jumped just as the first yelling seaman lunged to stop her.

The last thing she heard as she hit the water was Tanner's voice over the ship's speaker system warning the crew that the ship was about to explode.

"THAT LOOKS LIKE more than engine pollution, Seth Lewis said, watching the tendrils of smoke escape the Nilian vessel. "If it's a fire, this could be really bad."

"Sonofabitch!" Bartley yelled. "Some guy just jumped overboard."

Lewis grabbed his binoculars. "Correction. We've got a woman overboard."

"Can't ignore a damsel in distress," the pilot said. "Who wants to be the first hero of the day?"

"Whoa!" Bartley yelled, leaning over and out the side of the chopper. "The ship is raining bodies now. Looks like the whole crew is going overboard. Somebody knows something."

"Smoke's heavier," Jeff said. "Gotta be a fire on board and someone must have tipped the crew off as to what they're hauling."

"Thank goodness for that," Lewis said.

Bartley pulled on a wet suit. "Woman overboard is waving for help. Let's rock and roll." He leaned toward the pilot. "Hover low over the female. I'll shimmy down the ladder rope and get her and the guys can haul us up and in."

"Gotcha," the pilot shouted. "Hold on tight. I may have to pull back fast. Don't want to get caught in the updraft if that ship blows."

Things happened quickly after that. Within a couple of minutes, Bartley had the woman in his arms and was being pulled in. They'd barely made it back into the chopper when the first explosion hit the ship and started a chain reaction. By the time the fireworks stopped, there were huge holes in the back third of the ship and flames were shooting fifty feet or more into the air.

Lewis knelt by the side of the woman and helped her out of her life jacket. "You don't look Hispanic," he said.

"I'm not. I'm Georgette Delacroix, junior prosecuting attorney with the New Orleans District Attorney's Office.''

''How in the world did you wind up on that ship?''

''I was abducted.''

''Were there other Americans on the boat?''

''At least one. Tanner Harrison.''

Both Lewis and Bartley let out low whistles.

''Can you believe that guy?'' Lewis said. ''You might know he'd get the best seat in the house for the action.''

But there was no envy in his voice. They were all too keenly aware that the man in the best seat might not have gotten out alive.

I'LL MEET YOU LATER.

Tanner had promised that, and Georgette had held on to that vow ever since she'd jumped from the boat. She was still holding on, but apprehension had her so shaky she'd had difficulty uncorking a bottle of wine.

She glanced at her watch for the millionth time. Ten minutes before eight. Four and a half hours since she'd been rescued by the helicopter.

Taking the glass of wine she'd just poured, she opened the French doors and stepped out to the balcony. The city looked the same as it had a week ago, but nothing felt the same. The secret agent with the fierce sense of duty toward his job and his daughter had touched her heart in ways that had changed her forever.

All her life, she'd been afraid of romantic relationships, afraid to risk falling in love only to have the guy walk out of her life because he couldn't deal with the gift—the way her father had walked out on her and her mother.

But she'd fallen hard for Tanner, and it had been the gift that had brought them together.

The phone rang and Georgette's heart leapt to her throat. She checked the caller ID. Isabella again. Georgette had ignored her calls all afternoon, determined to keep the line open for Tanner. This time she gave in to the persistent ring and answered. "Hello."

"Georgette. Where have you been? I've been calling all afternoon, worried sick about you."

The adrenaline rush dissolved in disappointment. "Why were you worried, Momma?"

"I had a vision of you. You were on a ship that exploded. It was so real. I don't know if I've ever been so afraid."

"It's okay, Momma. I'm fine."

"You don't sound fine. You sound upset. This has to do with the man you told me about the other day, doesn't it?"

"Was he in the vision?"

"No. A mother just knows these things. Are you in love with this man?"

Georgette started to lie, then decided not to bother. Her mother always saw right through her lies anyway. "Yes, I am."

"Does he love you?"

"I don't know. We haven't talked about it."

"He doesn't have to say it for you to know. I knew with your father long before he did, the same way I knew he was leaving. I knew he couldn't deal with the gift."

"Did you miss him terribly when he left?"

"Yes."

"Were you sorry that you'd married him?"

"At first, but not now. How could I be? I have wonderful memories of the two of us together. And I have you."

They only talked a minute more, but Georgette stood on the balcony for a long time after breaking the connection, staring into the night and thinking of Isabella's words.

Her mother had lost the man she loved and ended up alone. But at least she had her memories. That's all Georgette was asking for tonight—a chance to make memories with Tanner. She wanted him in her arms, in her bed and in her heart.

But mostly she just wanted to know that he was safe.

After another half hour of waiting for her phone to ring, she went back inside, slipped out of her shoes and clothes and stepped into her second hot shower of the evening. There didn't seem to be enough soap or water to get rid of the stench of the boat and the river.

She explored her body with her fingers as the spray cascaded her head and shoulders and ran in rivulets between her breasts and down her abdomen.

We should have made love.

Tanner might have been under the influence of the drug when he made that statement, but it was true all the same.

She'd just worked a lather of shampoo in her hair when she heard the knock at her door. Her heart somersaulted out of control. It had to be Tanner. It just had to be.

She didn't bother with rinsing, just grabbed a towel, wrapped it around her and ran to the door. She peeked through the peephole, then jerked the door open and launched herself into Tanner's arms.

She didn't even notice when the towel slipped and fell to the floor.

THE GREETING took Tanner by surprise. He'd been dead tired and emotionally drained when he'd stopped at his place to shower and change into clean clothes, so exhausted he'd practically fallen asleep at a traffic light driving over here. But now his body had come screaming back to life.

"Oh, Tanner. You jumped. You're safe. You're here."

He didn't bother with an answer, just let his lips find hers while his hands found the rest of her slick, wet body. He touched all the places he could reach with her locked in his arms. Her shoulders, her buttocks, the backs of her thighs, and all the while the kiss grew sweeter, hotter and wetter.

Fitting his hands under her buttocks, he lifted her a foot off the floor just to feel her body slide down his rock-hard erection.

"I'm all soapy," she whispered, pulling away as if she thought that mattered. "I need to rinse."

He picked her up and carried her to the bathroom, then set her down in the shower while he kicked out of his shoes and wiggled out of his clothes. He joined her under the pulsating spray, and the intoxicating miracle of it all hit again.

He'd panicked when he'd learned she'd been abducted and taken to the ship. He'd nearly gone crazy when the rescue attempt had been thwarted. He'd lived through hell when he'd thought he might have to stand by and do nothing while she was violated by Gonzalez and the other Scorpion thugs.

Now she was here and safe, and he wanted her with a hunger such as he'd never known before. This time he couldn't blame the savage desire on a drug. The magic was all Georgette.

He kissed her over and over, then touched his lips to her breasts, sucking each nipple while his hands caressed the soft, perfect mounds of flesh. He roamed her abdomen, then slipped a hand between her legs and caught the water that dripped from the dark curly hairs.

She moaned when he slipped his fingers inside her, arching toward him and writhing against him. She was hot and moist and he knew he couldn't hold off much longer. She touched him in all the right places and in all the right ways, as if she couldn't get enough of him. He damn sure couldn't get enough of her.

Finally when he could wait no longer, he pushed inside her and gasped from the thrill of it. Perfect, so perfect. Right down to the feel of her lips on his neck. And then he gave it up, lost his breath entirely as he climaxed in a burst of sexual energy and savage passion.

Georgette squealed in pleasure then clung to him tightly as the warm spray splashed over their passion-spent bodies.

"Oh, Tanner, that was good. You were good. So very good."

Words to thrill his soul and perch him up right on top of the world. No words of love or talk of forever. He was thankful for that.

He cared about Georgette, cared so much it frightened him, but vows of love and forever had never worked for him. They'd always led to disaster, and he wasn't nearly ready to face disaster with Georgette.

They stepped out of the shower and onto the plush white bath mat. He pulled a fluffy towel from the rack and gave every inch of her a brisk rubdown. By the time she was dry, he was all hot and bothered again.

But first, he had to tell her about Sebastion.

GEORGETTE PULLED ON a robe, then padded to the hall closet and took a flowered quilt from the top shelf. She had no idea what had turned Tanner so serious all of a sudden, but she wasn't ready to kill the loving mood. "We can spread this on the balcony and talk while lying beneath the stars," she said.

Tanner took the quilt. "Sounds good. Is it private?"

"Totally."

"Then don't bother with this." He tugged on the belt of her silk robe, loosened it and slipped it from her shoulders.

"You spread the quilt," she said. "I'll pour some wine. I have merlot or a cab."

"Merlot's good."

She watched him walk away, not nude as she was but barefoot and shirtless and looking incredibly sexy. Making love with him had been breathtaking. Having him here was wondrous. So wondrous that she hated to spoil the night with talk of anything but love.

Tanner was stretched out on his back, jeans unsnapped, his hands cradling the back of his head when she joined him on the balcony. She set the glasses on the floor and stretched out beside him.

"I heard all about your rescue from the river," Tanner said. "Your bravery impressed the hell out of my fellow agents."

"All I did was jump in the water. There wasn't a lot of bravery involved in that."

"They said you were cool and in control."

"I was scared to death, mostly worried about you. When did you jump?"

"Not soon enough."

"Don't tell me you were on the ship when it blew up?"

"Yes, but at the other end. Good thing I was still there. Several of the crewmen were injured when the first explosion hit. I helped them into life jackets and shoved them overboard before jumping myself."

"Always the hero."

"Not always."

She heard the hurt in his voice and knew he was thinking of Lily. He wouldn't rest until he found her. "What happened to Ricardo Gonzalez and his followers?"

"It's hard to say exactly. There was a lot of confusion at the rescue site. Our guys picked up some of the survivors. The Coast Guard picked up the rest. At least a dozen Hispanics with scorpion tattoos were accounted for. Indications are that Gonzalez wasn't one of them. It's likely he was blown up in that first explosion since he's the logical choice to have set fire to the smuggled weapons."

"Guess he considered that dying for his country."

"Or taking his own life before Black Death did it for him." Tanner raised to his elbows, took a sip of wine then turned to face her. "There was another development this afternoon, Georgette. I hate to have to tell you this, but you'll hear it as soon as you catch the news. Sebastion shot himself."

"Oh, no." She cringed and tried to swallow. "Is he..."

"No. He's not dead. His wife arrived at his office

and found him on the floor lying in a pool of blood. She called for an ambulance and had him rushed to the hospital. He's conscious, but critical.''

"Has he admitted anything?''

"Everything. The doctors advised him not to talk, but he insisted that he speak with the chief of police. He's admitted his involvement with Senegal and Maurice Gaspard and given enough incriminating evidence against them to keep them in prison for the rest of their lives. He even supplied the name of the group of felonious businessmen who supplied the illegal arms.''

She rolled the news over in her mind, still having trouble believing that Sebastion could have sunk so low. "What a turn of events. From powerful district attorney to attempted suicide to informer in a matter of hours.''

"Seems like even Sebastion had his breaking point,'' Tanner said. "He told his wife he knew that if he didn't break away, she and the kids would inevitably be drawn into the hell he'd created the same way you were drawn in.''

"Poor Louise. This must be so difficult for her.''

"Probably just the beginning of problems for her. But it's the end of Senegal's reign. He and his mob network are being rounded up and arrested by the local police as we speak.''

"That's quite an accomplishment. Your secret agency must be pleased. You did all you set out to do and even discovered how the Nilians were smuggling drugs into the country.''

"Found that out the hard way,'' Tanner admitted. "But then I learn most things the hard way.''

"Really? I thought you might have decided to take

another chew on the burlap bag before you came over tonight.''

''Nope. That arousal was all you.'' He ran his hand over her bare backside. ''Are you addictive as well?''

''Only one way to find out,'' she teased.

She scooted closer. Tanner set his glass back on the decking and took her in his arms. He hadn't mentioned their future as a couple, but even if he had, she still had the gift to contend with. Best to take this one moment at a time.

And moments with Tanner were heaven.

TANNER WOKE UP at four in the morning to the sound of his vibrating phone knocking against the bedside table. He grabbed it, then checked to see if it had wakened Georgette. She squirmed but didn't open her eyes.

Easing his legs from between the crisp sheets, he tiptoed across the room and into the hallway before taking the call.

''This is Marsha, Tanner—Juliana's sister.''

He swallowed the curse that flew to his lips. He had enough problems dealing with Juliana. He didn't need the rest of the family pointing out his sins. He opened the French door and walked onto the balcony.

''Did Juliana put you up to calling?''

''No. She doesn't know, and if she did, she wouldn't approve.''

''So what's so important that you woke me in the middle of the night.''

''It's ten in the morning here, and I just saw a news broadcast about a ship that was smuggling arms being blown up just outside New Orleans.''

''And you figured I was behind the smuggling?''

"No, of course not, but I know your history, Tanner. You've always been in the thick of some kind of action. I just want to make certain you haven't dragged Lily into your crime-fighting antics. Tell me she wasn't anywhere near that boat."

Damn. He hadn't even thought of that possibility. "No reason to think that she was."

"She's your daughter, Tanner. For once in your life, do something right by her. Find her."

"I'm trying. In spite of what you and your sister seem to think of my parenting skills, I love my daughter very much. Always have."

"Then why didn't you come to her seventeenth birthday party as she begged you to? If you had, none of this would have happened."

"Wait a minute. Let's keep things straight here. I wanted to come. Juliana said Lily had changed her mind and didn't want me there."

The pause lasted so long that Tanner checked to see if the connection had been lost. When Marsha spoke again, her tone had softened. "Are you sure?"

"I'm positive. So you tell me. Why did Juliana lie about that? I know she hates me, but why would she hurt Lily?"

"I never thought she'd go that far, but you lived with her for seven years, Tanner. You know what she's like."

"I lived with her. I never understood her."

"She has psychological problems. You surely knew that much?"

"Are we talking about the same Juliana that I was married to? Perfect mother. Long-suffering wife."

"Don't tell me this comes as a surprise to you?"

"More of a shock. What kind of psychological problems?"

"Her current psychologist calls her condition a bipolar disorder, but she's had several diagnoses throughout the years for basically the same behaviors. The medicine helps—when she stays on it."

"Why wouldn't she?"

"She's Juliana."

"So she makes up lies about me and feeds them to our daughter."

"Evidently. Life's been tough on Lily, Tanner. We've all tried to help, but we couldn't take your place. She needed the stability of having a father in her life."

"I never knew. I mean… I thought…"

"All that matters is that you find her, Tanner. She ran away to America to be with you, so you find her and keep her safe."

"I'm trying. And thanks for the call—though it's about ten years too late."

THE CEMETERY was eerie in the predawn grayness, more creepy and frightening than even the swamp had been. The graves were all above ground, in mausoleums. Houses of the dead. Lily shivered and drew further inside herself.

Tony was leading her along. He'd cut the ropes that bound her ankles when he'd taken her out of the trunk of the car, but her hands were still tied behind her back. And the hard, terrifying barrel of a pistol pressed into the back of her head at the nape of her neck.

"Almost there," Tony said, giving her another shove.

"Almost where?"

"To a special place I've planned just for you. Got all the modern comforts. A stone pillow. Hot and cold running spiders. Scorpions. Decaying bodies."

Her stomach pitched and turned. He was going to leave her here, locked inside one of these haunted brick structures. Leave her with the dead bodies until she was one of them. Already she could swear there were cold, skeletal fingers knotting around her throat and cutting off her breath.

"Don't leave me here. I'll do whatever you say. But please, don't leave me here in a house of the dead."

"Too late for begging, you crazy, eye-poking whore. You may as well go back to being a bitchy wildcat."

Tony stopped at one of the structures, took a gun from his pocket and shot the lock from the thick wooden door. The crack of the bullet was almost deafening, but the cemetery was desolate, deserted of life and the dead wouldn't hear.

"Don't worry, Lily. You won't last long. This one is specially built. Airtight. Keeps out the evil spirits. Keeps in the dead. The Senegal family is very suspicious. They worry about things like that."

He took a new lock from his pocket, then opened the door of the crypt and shoved her inside. Something cold and foreign climbed her spine. A scream ripped from her parched throat and she kicked at Tony, hoping he'd shoot her now.

But he just slammed the door shut and left her in the pitch-black swirl of never-ending darkness. A huge spider fell from the low ceiling and onto her face. Its hairy legs skittered across her eyelids. An omen of all the terror to come.

She had no casket. She had no tombstone. But she'd entered everyone's worst nightmare.

She was buried alive.

Chapter Sixteen

Tony kept looking behind him as he walked the twisted paths that meandered through the ancient cemetery. The uneasiness had nothing to do with superstition or fear of the dead. It didn't relate to Lily, either. She was just another whore who'd made his hit list.

It was the lack of control that made him anxious. The network had been shut down completely. No one was giving orders; no one was taking them. He didn't dare make a phone call to Jerome or Gaspard for fear their phone lines were tapped and his location would be traced.

It had all happened so fast. One minute they were celebrating victory. The arms were on the ship and the deal was done. The continued drug supply was assured.

The next minute Sebastion Primeaux was lying in the ICU, squealing like a cat with its tail caught in a swinging door. Now the police were swarming like flies, making arrests and carting everyone off to jail.

It wouldn't blow over this time, either. No judge would pull a few strings and get them off. Senegal and his mob were down for the count. Tony had no intention of going down with the rest of them.

He had a stash of drugs locked in the trunk of his car, enough to pull in a quarter of a million bucks on the open market. There were lots of countries where a man could live like a king on that. All he had to do was get the drugs and himself out of New Orleans and over to the small airport outside of Biloxi where a chartered plane was waiting to fly him to Mexico.

His ride should be here within the hour, the guy Senegal had just brought on board and who, with luck, the cops didn't know about yet. Tony's only regret was that he wouldn't get to stuff Tanner Harrison in the tomb with his daughter. The guy was obsessed with saving her, and obsessed men were the most dangerous.

The sun was peeking over the horizon now. No one could see him from the street, and he doubted anyone would be strolling through the desolate cemetery at sunrise. But he wouldn't take chances. He scrunched down behind a crumbling structure to wait for his contact.

Finally he let his mind settle on Lily. Encased in the tomb. Waiting to die. The thought brought Tony his first smile of the day.

GEORGETTE WOKE and padded into the living room, searching for Tanner. She was relieved to smell perking coffee and to see the doors to the balcony open. She hadn't wanted to think he'd just woken up and left without telling her goodbye.

She joined him on the balcony and touched a hand to his broad, bare shoulder. He didn't turn to face her, but slipped an arm around her waist.

"What are you doing up at sunrise?" he asked.

"Looking for you."

"I'm sorry. I couldn't sleep and didn't want to keep you awake with my tossing."

"You must have Lily on your mind."

"Thinking what a lousy father I am. Ex-CIA. Current secret agent. Yet I can't even find my own daughter."

"You're doing everything you can, and it's not as if you forced her to come to America or get involved with Senegal and Gaspard."

"According to Juliana's sister, I'm to blame for all of it."

She listened as he told her about the phone conversation. Poor guy. He was being hammered from all sides.

"I've failed Lily all her life and now it's just more of the same."

"You didn't fail Lily. Juliana did that with her lies."

"I should have seen through them. I didn't. I never do. I always let down the people who need me most."

"Why do you say that?"

"Why shouldn't I say it? It's true."

He stared into space. His arm was still around her waist, but he was somewhere else, lost in memories that seemed to be tearing him apart.

She played with the question that haunted her own mind. She wasn't sure she wanted to hear the answer, but if they were ever going anywhere in their relationship, they couldn't let secrets stand between them.

"You said you'd loved one other woman besides Juliana," she said. "Is that who you let down?"

He nodded. "We were college sweethearts, had

talked about marriage since our second date. But first I had to fulfill my National Guard requirements with a six-month stint in active duty. She wanted to marry before I left. I refused.''

''Why?''

''I wanted a job first, a steady income.''

''That sounds reasonable.''

''But that wasn't all of it. I loved her but wasn't ready to be tied down to the responsibility of a wife and the kids she wanted to have right away.''

''Not being ready for marriage doesn't make you a failure, Tanner. You were young. You had your whole life in front of you.''

''Turned out she didn't have all that long. She was pregnant with our child. She didn't tell me, didn't want to saddle me with a child when I wasn't ready. Once I left, she went to some quack and had an abortion. She died from the resulting infection.''

And he was still feeling the responsibility of her death after all these years. It sounded unreasonable, yet she'd done much the same, had suffered from the sting of her father's rejection all her life. It was past time both of them let go of the old hurts.

''It was a long time ago, Tanner. You may have made a mistake, but you didn't even know about the baby.''

''That's a cop-out.'' He turned away. ''The same way my actions with Lily were a cop-out. I should have gone to London and insisted on seeing her. Instead I bought Juliana's lies and let my daughter believe I didn't care.''

''But you do care. You have to let go of the guilt, Tanner. It's destroying your chance to…'' His chance to love again. The words were on her tongue, but she didn't say them.

"I'm bad news, Georgette. If you stick around long enough, you'll make that discovery for yourself."

She couldn't reach him, and it hurt too much to watch him destroying himself like this. She slipped from his arms and went back to bed, though she imagined sleep was over for the night.

The trance started the second she climbed between the sheets.

FEAR STOLE her breath and rattled in her dry, burning lungs. She could see the man, hunkered down by the all-too-familiar tomb with the series of Xs painted on it. Only he wasn't really a man. He was part devil, the rest some evil-incarnate substance that had escaped the soul of a human.

Slowly the image of the man evaporated, and she sank into a blackness so deep that there was no difference whether her eyes were open or closed. She tried to move, but her legs were sluggish and cumbersome and her hands were bound by scratchy ropes that dug into her flesh.

The smell of decay clogged her nostrils and seeped into every pore of her body. She couldn't see so much as a shadow, but she had the feeling that ghostly spirits were hovering over her and stealing all the oxygen for themselves.

She tried to swallow, but her mouth was too dry. All of her was dry, parched like toast that had been left under the broiler too long. Water. She needed water.

Something wrapped around her, snakelike, squeezing her lungs. Her muscles went taut and she bit her bottom lip so hard that she tasted blood. But the thing didn't let go. Its cold, clenching hands were around her, ready to lift her and carry her away.

Finally the panic overrode the paralyzing effects of the fear and she kicked wildly and screamed.

THE MUG Tanner was holding when he heard the scream slipped from his hands and clattered against the counter, showering the kitchen with coffee and pottery fragments.

He took off running, reaching Georgette in seconds. She was ghostly pale and shivering, and a trickle of blood oozed from her bottom lip. Apprehension twisted his stomach into knots as he dropped to the edge of the bed and took her in his arms.

"It's okay. I'm here. You're safe."

"It's not okay, Tanner. Not this time."

"Is it Lily? Is she alive?"

"Just barely."

His lungs constricted, and the next question stuck in his throat. He was afraid to ask it, horrified that the answer would be as it had always been before. "Do you know where she is?"

"In a cemetery."

"That's too vague. What cemetery? We have to know what cemetery."

"St. Louis, Number One. I saw the grave of Marie Laveau in the visions."

"Are you certain?"

"Yes. My mother was fascinated with the legendary Voodoo Queen. She took me to her burial place often."

St. Louis, Number One: one of the many cities of the dead scattered about New Orleans. Places where bodies were tucked away in above-ground tombs so that the high water level wouldn't push them out of the graves and wash them away.

And now some madman had taken Lily there. "Tell me exactly where the tomb is."

"I can't give you directions without a cemetery map, but I can show it to you."

He started to stand, but she pulled him back down beside her.

"There's more, Tanner."

More. Always more, and never good. "What now?"

"Lily isn't just in the cemetery. She's locked inside one of the tombs."

The horror burned into his mind. His Lily was buried alive. He retreated inside himself, let his memories slide back to the time when Lily was a little girl, playing in the park, loving the big slides, but never wanting to go through the enclosed tunnels. She'd always hated tight places.

She had to be terrified now. He had to hurry and find her. "Is she in Marie Laveau's tomb?"

"No, but I think she's somewhere nearby. There was a man there. I didn't see his face well enough to be certain, but I think it was Tony Arsenault."

A surge of adrenaline pushed through the terror, and Tanner jumped from the bed and ran for his phone. Georgette caught his arm as he started to punch in Burke's number.

"What are you doing?" she demanded.

"Calling for help. We can't search every mausoleum by ourselves."

"You can't find her that way, either. If you call in the police or your agency, the cemetery will become chaotic and the visions will never come. We won't stand a chance of finding Lily in the hundreds of crypts before it's too late."

"Do you have a better suggestion?"

"We'll go there together, just the two of us. Give the images a chance."

"You want me to depend on your visions when you admit yourself that they never come on demand?"

"I can't explain it, but they'll come this time. They want us to find Lily."

"I can't do it, Georgette. I appreciate all your help, but I can't wait on some fickle vision. We have to do this my way."

"Without the visions to guide us to her quickly, she'll die. She's so very close to death now."

"How can you be sure of that?"

Georgette trembled and hugged her arms around her chest. "Because I was in the crypt with her. And because death has a feeling all its own."

THERE WAS LITTLE TRAFFIC that time of the morning and it took under ten minutes to drive to the old cemetery just outside the French Quarter. Tanner parked on the street and took off running behind Georgette through the twisted maze of sepulchers. The cemetery dated back to the late 1700s, and the mere age of most of the brick and stucco structures gave the place a disintegrating, decaying appearance that added to his dread.

"That's the tomb of Marie Laveau," Georgette said, panting for breath and pointing to a tall, rectangular tomb with burned candles, small trinkets and coins scattered around it. "The man was crouched behind it as if he were hiding."

Tanner didn't doubt her recollection of the image, but there was no one there now. "I'll give the images five minutes," he said, "then I'm calling for help and I'm going to start ripping these rotting shells to the ground with my bare hands if that's what it takes."

She moved away from him, as if she thought his threats were going to offend the psychic spirits that seemed to control Lily's fate. He didn't follow, but walked in the other direction, cringing at the sound of a rusty cross creaking in the slight breeze.

His insides tied themselves into frayed knots. Lily was here somewhere and he was standing around waiting for some psychic phenomena that seemed to specialize in tormenting him. He listened for any unusual sounds as he walked, a knocking or banging inside one of the tombs—or a call for help.

He raised his hand to beat on the door of one of the more decrepit tombs, then stopped when he spied the figure on the path to his left. Tanner lunged for cover, then peered around the side of the structure for a better look. Probably a groundskeeper—or a homeless man who wasn't afraid of sleeping with the dead.

But it was neither. It was Mason Bartley. His presence here could only mean one thing. Fury swelled so fast and furiously that it felt as if Tanner's head had left his body and gone into orbit. He drew his gun, then struggled to control his rage. Shooting Bartley wouldn't save Lily.

He waited until his partner was only a few feet away, then held the semiautomatic in front of him and stepped from behind the tomb.

"I thought I smelled a rat."

"Harrison. What are doing here, man?"

"I'm here to find my daughter. I know she's in one of the tombs so start talking, Bartley, before I splatter your brains all over the cemetery."

"You got this all wrong. And keep your voice down," Mason said, scanning the area around them.

"I don't have anything wrong, Bartley. I knew you couldn't change, but I never thought you'd sink this low."

"I didn't. I'm on your side. You gotta trust me on this."

"Trust slime? Putrid, debased slime with Senegal's blood money eating away at your soul? I don't think so. Now, where's Lily?"

"I don't know. That's the truth. I came here to try and get information about her, the same as you."

"You never stop lying, do you? Drop your gun and throw it to the ground."

"You need to rethink this, Tanner," Mason pleaded, dropping his gun.

"Kick the gun over here, then spread your legs and place your hands on the wall of that tomb next to you."

Tanner searched him. The one gun was all he was packing, but he was carrying a knife in a boot holster. Tanner took it and tossed it into the dirt path. Holding his gun a few inches from Bartley's head, he pulled back the hammer. "This is the last time I'm asking, Bartley. Where's Lily?"

"I don't know. Tony Arsenault..."

"Did someone call my name?"

Tanner spun around. Tony was standing a few feet away, holding the butt of an automatic whose barrel was pressed into Georgette's right temple.

Sonofabitch. He'd walked right into this. He pointed his gun at Tony, though he knew it was a bluff. He couldn't kill Tony before Tony got off a bullet and killed Georgette.

"Nice little party we got here," Tony said. "No one's missing but Daddy's little whore. Too bad. She was nice, Harrison, really nice. Glad I got a piece of that while she was still breathing."

It was all Tanner could do not to pull the trigger, but he held steady. "Lily's still breathing and she will be, long after you're not."

"You shoot me, I shoot the lady. And you still won't have your daughter."

Tony was right. He held all the cards. And he had Bartley to back him up. Tanner met Georgette's gaze, hoping to give her some reassurance, though he doubted she'd buy it. He'd expected to see fear in her eyes, but instead they were glazed as if she were on drugs or intoxicated—or falling into a trance.

Not now. Please not now. Tony would have no idea what was going on and would probably shoot her on the spot if she tried to break away or started screaming.

Everything was skidding out of Tanner's control. He'd made so many mistakes in his life, but he couldn't lose this time. He loved Lily with all his heart. And then there was Georgette. He couldn't begin to understand his feelings for her, but he couldn't lose her like this.

He'd never needed a break the way he did now. He needed Tony to foul up. Lose his concentration. Make one errant move.

Georgette was falling deeper into the trance. She'd

turned ghostly white and her lips were trembling. She began to sway.

Tony grabbed her arm. "You move again, and you're dead."

Bartley stooped and picked up the pistol he'd dropped a few minutes ago. "Looks like you waited too long, Tony."

"We still got time."

"Not anymore. Look behind you. Tanner must have called in backup. We're surrounded by cops."

Tony jerked around just as Georgette took off running down one of the twisting alleys. He pointed his gun to shoot, but Tanner shot first. Tony bolted backward and fell to the ground.

Tanner looked around, then stared at Bartley. "There aren't any cops?"

"Naw. Just a couple of Confidential agents and a dead mob hit man. I suggest you follow your psychic girlfriend. My guess is she's heading for your daughter."

Tanner took off at a dead run, getting to the mausoleum a second after Georgette did. She fell against the structure, then knelt beside it, tears rolling down her cheeks. Tanner didn't wait for further explanation. He shot off the lock and kicked the door open.

All he could see was dark shadows. Nothing moved. No one called out. What if this was all a mistake? What if the visions had played a horrible, heartbreaking trick?

"Lily. It's Daddy. Are you in here?"

"Yes."

He shuddered as he moved into the darkness, picked her up and cradled her in his arms the way he'd done when she was just a baby. Nothing had ever felt so good.

"You found me. I didn't think you could. Not in the tomb."

"I had help. Lots of terrific help."

Bartley and Georgette were standing there when he carried her into the sunlight.

Lily smiled weakly and put her arms around his neck. Georgette wept openly. Bartley kept blinking as though the sun was blinding him even though he was standing in the shade. Tanner just kept walking, stunned to silence by the miracle of it all.

Epilogue

Two weeks later

What had started out as an informal gathering to toast their success in stopping the arms shipment to Nilia had evolved into a first-class celebration. Burke had booked a private dining room at Commander's Palace Restaurant and invited the wives of the agents and two guests of honor—Lily and Georgette.

Though he'd kept in touch by phone, it was the first time Tanner had seen any of the agents or Georgette since the morning he'd rescued Lily from the tomb. His daughter had a lot of emotional scars after almost two months of living in captivity or on the run, and this time he wanted to make sure he was there for her.

He'd taken her directly to the hospital for a thorough checkup and gotten the news from the doctor even before he heard it from Lily. In spite of it all, she was still a virgin.

She'd started out serving drinks for Madam Dupre at Gaspard's bordello, and had only been with a few men. In those instances, she'd followed the advice of one of the other call girls and slipped a powder into their first drink instead of the Category Five.

Tanner was grateful she'd never actually been violated by one of the johns who'd come to her room. Not that he wouldn't still love her every bit as much, but it was less violation she'd had to suffer. She'd been through far too much as it was, mostly because she'd been in the wrong place at the wrong time.

Tony had had on a mask when he'd shot Madam Dupre and Jack Smith, a bartender who was sending her clients. When he'd thought he was home free, he'd yanked off the mask. That's when he'd spotted Lily watching from the shadows and realized she'd witnessed the killings.

And that had started her trip to hell and back.

You'd never know it tonight. She was radiant. Her face had color again and her long blond hair was clean and shiny. She'd never be as innocent as she'd been before the ordeal, but she was happy and rediscovering her zest for life.

And she had a new best friend. Tanner had gotten Becky Lane admitted to a group home for runaway girls and helped her find a job. She'd be back in school next year, but in the meantime, she and Lily spent hours on the phone and Becky stopped by for frequent visits.

"Looks like everyone is here except Georgette," Burke said, once the group was seated at the dinner table. "She is still coming, isn't she?"

"As far as I know." It hit him how much he'd looked forward to seeing her again.

The chatter continued around him, easy talk, interrupted by lots of laughter and the soft tinkle of champagne glasses. The noise stopped when the door opened and Georgette stepped inside.

For a moment, Tanner just stared, mesmerized. He'd never seen her look bad, but she was dazzling tonight—sexy and elegant and so damn seductive that he had a hard time getting air into his lungs.

The shimmery red cocktail dress fit to perfection, revealing a hint of cleavage and baring the smooth flesh of her narrow shoulders. She wore no jewelry at all. Didn't need it. She was the gem.

Finally he got his wits about him enough to push back from the table, stand and welcome her to the group and hold out the chair next to him. Once they were seated, he leaned over and put his mouth close to her ear. "You look good enough to eat, counselor."

"Then save room for dessert."

The invitation sent shudders of anticipation along every nerve ending before settling in his crotch. Too bad this wasn't just about sex. He could have handled that easily. But Georgette haunted his mind and messed with his heart.

Bottom line—she still scared him big-time.

GEORGETTE HAD BEEN EXCITED about the prospect of dinner with Tanner and Lily and his buddies from New Orleans Confidential, especially now that they trusted her so much they'd even let Tanner tell her the name of the group. But though the food had been exceptional, the evening hadn't gone as well as she'd hoped. The other women, except for Lily, were all wives. Georgette was...

That was the problem. She wasn't sure what she was. A friend? A one-night stand? Someone Tanner had needed for a time but didn't need any longer? All of the above?

She understood his desire to spend time with his daughter. Lily had been weak, dehydrated and suffering from emotional trauma. But it had been two weeks and Tanner hadn't come to Georgette's once. Worse, he hadn't said he missed her or talked of the night they'd made love.

She couldn't get a handle on his feelings and she had too much of a handle on hers. She was in love with him, so much in love that she'd started trying to convince herself that they could have a life together, that the gift wouldn't matter with a man like Tanner.

But obviously something mattered. She was about to tell him she had to go when Conrad Burke stood and tapped his coffee spoon against the edge of his after-dinner brandy.

"I'm not much for speeches," he said, "but we should say something to justify putting this on our expense account, so I'll make this brief and to the point. You are one hell of a bunch of guys. We had a task and you not only succeeded at it but you got a dangerous drug-dealing mob organization off the streets, took out an underage prostitution ring and saved a beautiful damsel in distress. Can we get a hand for the damsel who's no longer in distress?"

He motioned Lily to stand. She turned to her dad first and beamed. "Thanks, especially to you, Daddy. And to Mason Bartley, the handsome agent whose bravery and dedication went far beyond the call of duty." She grinned. "He paid me to say that."

They all laughed, and someone asked if she was staying in America for a while.

"Yes. I'm going to live with my dad and attend

the University of New Orleans. I'm not sure what I want to be when I graduate, but right now I'm leaning toward law enforcement. You never know, I might just join the Confidential team one day." That brought more applause and a few cheers.

"And there's one more beautiful woman among us who deserves special attention," Burke said. "Georgette Delacroix, the woman who found the key to unlock the puzzle. I've already tried to sign her up. She turned me down. Take a bow, Georgette, but not too much of one. Bartley will fall into his bread pudding souffle trying to check out your cleavage."

She stood and managed a smile. "I would have joined up, but those truck-driving uniforms have no style," Georgette said, trying to keep things as light as Burke had, though she didn't feel light at all. "But I'm glad I could help. If you ever need a good attorney, look me up."

Burke made a few more announcements before Wiley Longbottom, the retired Confidential director who was recovering from a Category Five-induced heart attack, got up and said a few words. It was clear that the guys both loved and respected him.

"And last but not least," Burke said, "we have a special presentation from Mason Bartley to Tanner Harrison."

Mason stood and held up a square of posterboard with a holograph of a leopard attached. When you viewed it from one angle, the leopard had all its spots. When you viewed it from another, they disappeared completely.

"Just a reminder, partner," Bartley said, looking right at Tanner. "Spots are only skin deep."

"Ouch! But I guess I deserved that. I never even

suspected you were working as a double agent.'' Tanner went over and clapped Bartley on the shoulder.
''You still don't know how to tail a car, though,'' he
joked. ''But I'm willing to teach you if you tell me
how you got Tony Arsenault to fall so easily for a
movie line like, 'We're surrounded by cops.'''

''It's all in the delivery, man. And when you got
it, you've just got it.''

Georgette stood and slipped out the door as if she
were going to the ladies room. It was a Confidential
night. She wasn't part of the group and likely never
would be. Better to go home now and forget all about
Tanner Harrison. While she was at it, she'd forget that
fire was hot and ice was cold and that the psychic
Georgette Delacroix was never going to get the man.

TANNER SAW GEORGETTE leave and was hit with a
wave of panic that pulled him right out of the Kodak
moment he was having with Bartley. He stood still
until Marilyn finished getting her picture, then took
off after Georgette, having no clue what he was going
to say or why he was feeling so desperate.

He caught up with her on the stairs leading to the
first floor. He grabbed her arm to slow her down.
''Why did you run off?''

She jerked from his grasp. ''I didn't run off. Dinner
was finished. It was time to go.''

''Without saying goodbye?''

She sighed, but kept walking, this time out the front
door of the restaurant. ''Goodbyes are hard for me.''

A smiling young man appeared at Tanner's elbow.
''Can I get your car, sir?''

''No.''

"You can get mine," Georgette said, handing him the parking stub.

"Forget her car. She's not leaving yet." This time when Tanner grabbed her arm, he held on and tugged her away from the front door of the restaurant. "I don't know what's going on, but I want straight answers."

"You haven't asked a question."

Right. He hadn't, and there was only one on his mind. He couldn't believe he was even thinking it, but it was there, pushing to the forefront. Bad as he hated to admit it, the question had been dancing around ever since that morning in the cemetery when he'd seen Tony's pistol pressed against Georgette's temple.

"What's the question, Tanner?"

If he thought about this too long, he'd never get it right. Best just to blurt it out. "Will you marry me?"

She took a step backward and looked him in the eye. "What did you say?"

He hesitated. "I think I asked you if you'd marry me."

"You think?"

Here it was, one of those moments that changed your life forever. Let it pass, and… Let it pass and Georgette would walk right out of his life.

"I don't think. I know. Will you marry me, Georgette?"

"Why?"

"Because…" He took a deep breath. Might as well admit the truth to her even though he'd fought admitting it to himself. "Because I love you and I want to spend the rest of my life with you. I know it's sudden, and you don't have to answer right away, but

I lost ten years of my daughter's life because I didn't have sense enough to claim it. I don't want to miss another second of loving you.''

"Oh, Tanner...I love you, too!" She was on the verge of throwing herself into his arms, then stopped. "What about the gift?"

"What about it?"

"It's not going away. I have to live with it. If you marry me, you'll have to live with it, too."

"And you'll have to live with my being a secret agent. It's probably a fair trade-off. Besides the gift brought us together and it saved Lily's life." He took her hands in his, more afraid than ever, but this time the fear was that she was going to say no. "You haven't answered."

"Yes! The answer is yes, yes, yes." She did that jump into the air and the cheerleader moves again. And they got to him again.

He pulled her into his arms and kissed her hungrily to the applause of the onlookers. Tanner gave them a thumbs-up, sure that nothing in his life had ever felt this right before.

"One more thing to clear up, Tanner, before we go too far."

"Is there always one more thing with you?"

"Could be. I'm an attorney. We like everything spelled out. I don't want to have children. I won't pass the gift on, but I might want to adopt. How would you feel about that?"

Children. He hadn't thought about that. But... "Why not? I might even do it right this time."

Tanner held her close while visions of Georgette danced in his mind. He wasn't psychic, but he knew good fortune when it stared him in the face. His daughter was safe. He loved a woman who loved him back. He was on the team of the best damn secret agency in the world.

And three out of three was a winner every time.

HARLEQUIN®
INTRIGUE®

Someone had infiltrated the insular realm of the Colby Agency....

INTERNAL AFFAIRS

The line between attraction and protection has vanished in these two brand-new investigations.

Look for these back-to-back books by

DEBRA WEBB

October 2004
SITUATION: OUT OF CONTROL

November 2004
PRIORITY: FULL EXPOSURE

Available at your favorite retail outlet.

HARLEQUIN®
Live the emotion™

www.eHarlequin.com

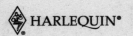
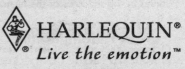

eHARLEQUIN.com
The Ultimate Destination for Women's Fiction

For **FREE online reading,** visit
www.eHarlequin.com now and enjoy:

Online Reads
Read **Daily** and **Weekly** chapters from
our Internet-exclusive stories by your
favorite authors.

Interactive Novels
Cast your vote to help decide how these
stories unfold...then stay tuned!

Quick Reads
For shorter romantic reads, try our
collection of Poems, Toasts, & More!

Online Read Library
Miss one of our online reads?
Come here to catch up!

Reading Groups
Discuss, share and rave with other
community members!

For great reading online,
visit www.eHarlequin.com today!

INTONL04

If you enjoyed what you just read,
then we've got an offer you can't resist!

Take 2 bestselling
love stories FREE!

Plus get a FREE surprise gift!

Clip this page and mail it to Harlequin Reader Service®

IN U.S.A.	IN CANADA
3010 Walden Ave.	P.O. Box 609
P.O. Box 1867	Fort Erie, Ontario
Buffalo, N.Y. 14240-1867	L2A 5X3

YES! Please send me 2 free Harlequin Intrigue® novels and my free surprise gift. After receiving them, if I don't wish to receive anymore, I can return the shipping statement marked cancel. If I don't cancel, I will receive 4 brand-new novels each month, before they're available in stores! In the U.S.A., bill me at the bargain price of $4.24 plus 25¢ shipping and handling per book and applicable sales tax, if any*. In Canada, bill me at the bargain price of $4.99 plus 25¢ shipping and handling per book and applicable taxes**. That's the complete price and a savings of at least 10% off the cover prices—what a great deal! I understand that accepting the 2 free books and gift places me under no obligation ever to buy any books. I can always return a shipment and cancel at any time. Even if I never buy another book from Harlequin, the 2 free books and gift are mine to keep forever.

181 HDN DZ7N
381 HDN DZ7P

Name	(PLEASE PRINT)	
Address	Apt.#	
City	State/Prov.	Zip/Postal Code

Not valid to current Harlequin Intrigue® subscribers.

Want to try two free books from another series?
Call 1-800-873-8635 or visit www.morefreebooks.com.

* Terms and prices subject to change without notice. Sales tax applicable in N.Y.
** Canadian residents will be charged applicable provincial taxes and GST.
All orders subject to approval. Offer limited to one per household.
® are registered trademarks owned and used by the trademark owner and or its licensee

INT04R   ©2004 Harlequin Enterprises Limited

Like a phantom in the night comes
a new promotion from

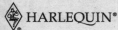
HARLEQUIN®

INTRIGUE®

GOTHIC ROMANCE

Beginning in August 2004, we offer you
a classic blend of chilling suspense and
electrifying romance, starting with....

A DANGEROUS INHERITANCE
LEONA KARR

And don't miss a spine-tingling Eclipse tale each month!

September 2004
MIDNIGHT ISLAND SANCTUARY
SUSAN PETERSON

October 2004
THE LEGACY OF CROFT CASTLE
JEAN BARRETT

November 2004
THE MAN FROM FALCON RIDGE
RITA HERRON

December 2004
EDEN'S SHADOW
JENNA RYAN

Available wherever Harlequin books are sold.
www.eHarlequin.com

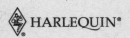

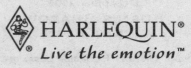